Oscar Fingal O'Flahertie Wills Wilde (16 October 1854 – 30 November 1900) was an Irish poet and playwright. After writing in different forms throughout the 1880s, he became one of London's most popular playwrights in the early 1890s. He is best remembered for his epigrams and plays, his novel The Picture of Dorian Gray, and the circumstances of his criminal conviction for homosexuality, imprisonment, and early death at age 46. Wilde's parents were successful Anglo-Irish intellectuals in Dublin. Their son became fluent in French and German early in life. At university, Wilde read Greats; he proved himself to be an outstanding classicist, first at Trinity College Dublin, then at Oxford. He became known for his involvement in the rising philosophy of aestheticism, led by two of his tutors, Walter Pater and John Ruskin. After university, Wilde moved to London into fashionable cultural and social circles. (Source: Wikipedia)

Literary works:
Ravenna (1878)
Poems (1881)
The Happy Prince and Other Stories (1888)
Lord Arthur Savile's Crime and Other Stories (1891)
A House of Pomegranates (1891)
Intentions (1891)
The Picture of Dorian Gray (1890)
The Soul of Man under Socialism (1891)
Lady Windermere's Fan (1892)
A Woman of No Importance (1893)
An Ideal Husband (1898)
The Importance of Being Earnest (1898)
De Profundis (1905)
The Ballad of Reading Gaol (1898)
The Portrait of Mr. W. H. (1889)

IMPRESSIONS OF AMERICA
&
LADY WINDERMERE'S FAN

Oscar Wilde

PRINCE CLASSICS

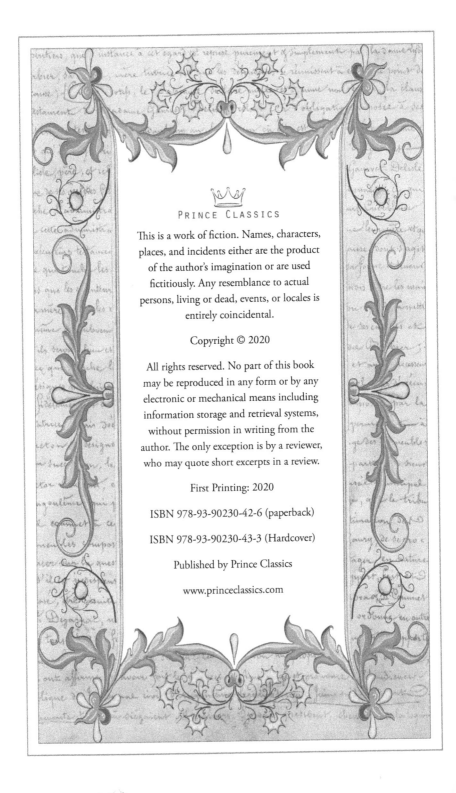

PRINCE CLASSICS

Copyright © 2020

First Printing: 2020

ISBN 978-93-90230-42-6 (paperback)

ISBN 978-93-90230-43-3 (Hardcover)

Published by Prince Classics

www.princeclassics.com

Contents

IMPRESSIONS OF AMERICA
&
LADY WINDERMERE'S FAN

IMPRESSIONS OF AMERICA

TO

WALTER LEDGER:

PIGNUS

AMICITIÆ.

IMPRESSIONS.

I.

LE JARDIN.

The lily's withered chalice falls
Around its rod of dusty gold,
And from the beech trees on the wold
The last wood-pigeon coos and calls.

The gaudy leonine sunflower
Hangs black and barren on its stalk,
And down the windy garden walk
The dead leaves scatter,—hour by hour.

Pale privet-petals white as milk
Are blown into a snowy mass;
The roses lie upon the grass,
Like little shreds of crimson silk.

II.

LA MER.

A white mist drifts across the shrouds,
A wild moon in this wintry sky
Gleams like an angry lion's eye
Out of a mane of tawny clouds.

The muffled steersman at the wheel

Is but a shadow in the gloom;—

And in the throbbing engine room

Leap the long rods of polished steel.

The shattered storm has left its trace

Upon this huge and heaving dome,

For the thin threads of yellow foam

Float on the waves like ravelled lace.

Oscar Wilde.

PREFACE.

Oscar Wilde visited America in the year 1882. Interest in the Æsthetic School, of which he was already the acknowledged master, had sometime previously spread to the United States, and it is said that the production of the Gilbert and Sullivan opera, "Patience,"[1] in which he and his disciples were held up to ridicule, determined him to pay a visit to the States to give some lectures explaining what he meant by Æstheticism, hoping thereby to interest, and possibly to instruct and elevate our transatlantic cousins.

He set sail on board the "Arizona" on Saturday, December 24th, 1881, arriving in New York early in the following year. On landing he was bombarded by journalists eager to interview the distinguished stranger. "Punch," in its issue of January 14th, in a happy vein, parodied these interviewers, the most amusing passage in which referred to "His Glorious Past," wherein Wilde was made to say, "Precisely—I took the Newdigate. Oh! no doubt, every year some man gets the Newdigate; but not every year does Newdigate get an Oscar."

At Omaha, where, under the auspices of the Social Art Club, Wilde delivered a lecture on "Decorative Art," he described his impressions of many American houses as being "illy designed, decorated shabbily, and in bad taste, filled with furniture that was not honestly made,   and was out of character." This statement gave rise to the following verses:—

What a shame and what a pity,

In the streets of London City

Mr. Wilde is seen no more.

Far from Piccadilly banished,

He to Omaha has vanished.

Horrid place, which swells ignore.

On his back a coat he beareth,

Such as Sir John Bennet weareth,

Made of velvet—strange array!

Legs Apollo might have sighed for,

Or great Hercules have died for,

His knee breeches now display.

Waving sunflower and lily,

He calls all the houses "illy

Decorated and designed."

For of taste they've not a tittle;

They may chew and they may whittle;

But they're all born colour-blind!

His lectures dealt almost exclusively with the subjects of Art and Dress Reform. In the course of one lecture he remarked that the most impressive room he had yet entered in America was the one in Camden Town where he met Walt Whitman. It contained plenty of fresh air and sunlight. On the table was a simple cruse of water. This led to a parody, in the style of Whitman, describing an imaginary interview between the two poets, which appeared in "The Century" a few months later. Wilde is called Narcissus and Whitman Paumanokides.

Paumanokides:—

Who may this be?

This young man clad unusually with loose locks, languorous, glidingly toward me advancing,

Toward the ceiling of my chamber his orbic and expressive eyeballs uprolling, and so on, to which Narcissus replies,

O clarion, from whose brazen throat,

Strange sounds across the seas are blown,

Where England, girt as with a moat,

A strong sea-lion sits alone!

Of the lectures which he delivered in America only one has been preserved, namely that on the English Renaissance. This was his first lecture, and it was delivered in New York on January 9th, 1882. According to a contemporary account in the "New York Herald" a distinguished and crowded audience assembled in Chickering Hall that evening to listen to one who "was well worth seeing, his short breeches and silk stockings showing to even better advantage upon the stage than in the gilded drawing-rooms, where the young Apostle has heretofore been seen in New York."[2]

On leaving the States in the "fall" of the year Wilde proceeded to Canada and thence to Nova Scotia, arriving in Halifax in the second week of October. Of his visit there we have no record except an amusing interview described in a local paper a few days later. He was dressed in a velvet jacket with an ordinary linen collar and neck tie and he wore trousers. "Mr. Wilde," the interviewer states, "was communicative and genial; he said he found Canada pleasant, but in answer to a question as to whether European or American women were the more beautiful, he dexterously evaded his querist."

As regards poetry he expressed his opinion that Poe was the greatest American poet, and that Walt Whitman, if not a poet, was a man who sounded a strong note, perhaps neither prose nor poetry, but something of his own that was "grand, original and unique."

During his tour in America Wilde "happened to find" himself (as he has himself described it), in Louisville, Kentucky. The subject he had selected to speak on was the Mission of Art in the Nineteenth Century. In the course of his lecture he had occasion to quote Keats' Sonnet on Blue "as an example of the poet's delicate sense of colour-harmonies." After the lecture there came round to see him "a lady of middle age, with a sweet gentle manner and most musical voice," who introduced herself as Mrs. Speed, the daughter of George Keats, and she invited the lecturer to come and examine the Keats manuscripts in her possession.

Some months afterwards when lecturing in California he received a letter from this lady asking him to accept the original manuscript of the sonnet which he had quoted.

Mention must be made of Wilde's first play, a drama in blank verse entitled "Vera, or the Nihilists." It had been arranged that, before his departure for America, this play should be performed at the Adelphi Theatre, London, with Mrs. Bernard Beere as the heroine, on Saturday, December 17th, 1881, but a few weeks before the date fixed for the first performance, the author decided to postpone the production "owing to the state of political feeling in England."

On his return to England in 1883 Wilde started on a lecturing tour, the first being to the Art Students of the Royal Academy at their Club in Golden Square on June 30th. Ten days later he spoke at Prince's Hall on his "Personal Impressions of America," and on subsequent occasions at Margate, Ramsgate and Southampton. On Monday, July 30th he lectured at Southport and on the following Thursday he went to Liverpool to welcome Mrs. Langtry on her return from America, and the same afternoon he left on his second visit to the States in order to superintend the rehearsals of "Vera," which it had been arranged to produce at the Union Square Theatre, New York, on August 20th following. The piece was not a success—it was, indeed, the only failure Wilde had. However, his next play, which he called his "Opus Secundum," also a blank verse tragedy, had a successful run in America in 1891. This was "The Duchess of Padua," played by Lawrence Barrett, under the title of "Guido Ferranti." This has not been seen in England, nor is it even possible for Wilde's admirers to read this early offspring of his pen, for only twenty copies were printed for acting purposes in America and of these but one is known to be in existence, in this country at least.

An authorised German translation was made by Max Meyerfeld and the first performance took place at the German Theatre in Hamburg about a year ago. An English version is advertised from a piratical publisher in Paris but it is only a translation from the German back into English.

Towards the end of September 1883 Oscar Wilde returned to England and immediately began "an all round lecturing tour," his first visit being to Wandsworth Town Hall on Monday,   September 24th, when he delivered to an enthusiastic audience a lecture on his "Impressions of America," which is contained in the following pages. He was dressed, a London paper of the time states, "in ordinary evening costume, and carried an orange-coloured silk handkerchief in his breast. He spoke with great fluency, in a voice now and then singularly musical, and only once or twice made a scarcely perceptible reference to notes." The lecture was under the auspices of a local Literary Society, and the principle residents of the district turned out "en masse." The Chairman, the Rev. John Park, in introducing the lecturer, said there were two reasons why he was glad to welcome him, and he thought his own feelings would be shared by the audience. They must all plead guilty to a feeling of curiosity, he hoped a laudable one, to see and hear Mr. Wilde for his own sake, and they were also glad to hear about America—a country which many might regard as a kind of Elysium.

On March 5th in the following year Wilde lectured at the Crystal Palace on his American experiences, and on April 26th he "preached his Gospel in the East-end," when it is recorded that his audience was not only delighted with his humour, but was "surprised at the excellent good sense he talked." His subject was a plea in favour of "art for schools," and many of his remarks about the English system of elementary education—with its insistence on "the population of places that no one ever wants to go to," and its "familiarity with the lives of persons who probably never existed"—were said to be quite worthy of Ruskin. A contemporary account adds that Wilde "showed himself a pupil of Mr. Ruskin's, too, in insisting   on the importance of every child being taught some handicraft, and in looking forward to the time when a boy would rather look at a bird or even draw it than throw "his customary stone!"

The British "gamin" has not made much progress in this respect during the last twenty years!

His lectures on "Dress," with the newspaper correspondence which they evoked, including some of Oscar Wilde's replies in his most characteristic vein, must be reserved for a future volume.

STUART MASON.

Oxford, January 1906.

1. First produced at the Opera Comique, April 23rd, 1881. Wilde was burlesqued as Reginald Bunthorne, a Fleshly Poet.

2. Wilde repeated this lecture throughout the States during his tour. At Rochester, on February 7th, he met with a most disorderly reception on the part of the College Students. Two days later Mr. Joaquin Miller, of St. Louis, wrote to Wilde saying that he had "read with shame about the behaviour of those ruffians." To this Wilde replied, "I thank you for your chivalrous and courteous letter," and in the course of his letter makes a more special attack on that critic whom he terms "the itinerant libeller of New England."

IMPRESSIONS OF AMERICA.

I fear I cannot picture America as altogether an Elysium—perhaps, from the ordinary standpoint I know but little about the country. I cannot give its latitude or longitude; I cannot compute the value of its dry goods, and I have no very close acquaintance with its politics. These are matters which may not interest you, and they certainly are not interesting to me.

The first thing that struck me on landing in America was that if the Americans are not the most well-dressed people in the world, they are the most comfortably dressed. Men are seen there with the dreadful chimney-pot hat, but there are very few hatless men; men wear the shocking swallow-tail coat, but few are to be seen with no coat at all. There is an air of comfort in the appearance of the people which is a marked contrast to that seen in this country, where, too often, people are seen in close contact with rags.

The next thing particularly noticeable is that everybody seems in a hurry to catch a train. This is a state of things which is not favourable to poetry or romance. Had Romeo or Juliet been in a constant state of anxiety about trains, or had their minds been agitated by the question of return-tickets, Shakespeare could not have given us those lovely balcony scenes which are so full of poetry and pathos.

America is the noisiest country that ever existed. One is waked up in the morning, not by the singing of the nightingale, but by the steam whistle. It is surprising that the sound practical sense of the Americans does not reduce this intolerable noise. All Art depends upon exquisite and delicate sensibility, and such continual turmoil must ultimately be destructive of the musical faculty.

There is not so much beauty to be found in American cities as in Oxford, Cambridge, Salisbury or Winchester, where are lovely relics of a beautiful age; but still there is a good deal of beauty to be seen in them now and then, but only where the American has not attempted to create it. Where the Americans have attempted to produce beauty they have signally failed. A remarkable characteristic of the Americans is the manner in which they have applied science to modern life.

This is apparent in the most cursory stroll through New York. In England an inventor is regarded almost as a crazy man, and in too many instances invention ends in disappointment and poverty. In America an inventor is honoured, help is forthcoming, and the exercise of ingenuity, the application of science to the work of man, is there the shortest road to wealth. There is no country in the world where machinery is so lovely as in America.

I have always wished to believe that the line of strength and the line of beauty are one. That wish was realised when I contemplated American machinery. It was not until I had seen the water-works at Chicago that I realised the wonders of machinery; the rise and fall of the steel rods, the symmetrical motion of the great wheels is the most beautifully rhythmic thing I have ever seen.[3] One is impressed in America, but not favourably impressed, by the inordinate size of everything. The country seems to try to bully one into a belief in its power by its impressive bigness.

I was disappointed with Niagara—most people must be disappointed with Niagara. Every American bride is taken there, and the sight of the stupendous waterfall must be one of the earliest, if not the keenest, disappointments in American married life. One sees it under bad conditions, very far away, the point of view not showing the splendour of the water. To appreciate it really one has to see it from underneath the fall, and to do that it is necessary to be dressed in a yellow oil-skin, which is as ugly as a mackintosh—and I hope none of you ever wears one. It is a consolation to know, however, that such an artist as Madame Bernhardt has not only worn that yellow, ugly dress, but has been photographed in it.

Perhaps the most beautiful part of America is the West, to reach which, however, involves a journey by rail of six days, racing along tied to an ugly tin-kettle of a steam engine. I found but poor consolation for this journey in the fact that the boys who infest the cars and sell everything that one can eat—or should not eat—were selling editions of my poems vilely printed on a kind of grey blotting paper, for the low price of ten cents.[4] Calling these boys on one side I told them that though poets like to be popular they desire to be paid, and selling editions of my poems without giving me a profit is dealing a blow at literature which must have a disastrous effect on poetical aspirants. The invariable reply that they made was that they themselves made a profit out of the transaction and that was all they cared about.

It is a popular superstition that in America a visitor is invariably addressed as "Stranger." I was never once addressed as "Stranger." When I went to Texas I was called "Captain"; when I got to the centre of the country I was addressed as "Colonel," and, on arriving at the borders of Mexico, as "General." On the whole, however, "Sir," the old English method of addressing people is the most common.

It is, perhaps, worth while to note that what many people call Americanisms are really old English expressions which have lingered in our colonies while they have been lost in our own country. Many people imagine that the term "I guess," which is so common in America, is purely an American expression, but it was used by John Locke in his work on "The Understanding," just as we now use "I think."[5]

It is in the colonies, and not in the mother country, that the old life of the country really exists. If one wants to realise what English Puritanism is—not at its worst (when it is very bad), but at its best, and then it is not very good—I do not think one can find much of it in England, but much can be found about Boston and Massachusetts. We have got rid of it. America still preserves it, to be, I hope, a short-lived curiosity.

San Francisco is a really beautiful city. China Town, peopled by Chinese labourers, is the most artistic town I have ever come across. The people—strange, melancholy Orientals, whom many people would call common, and they are certainly very poor—have determined that they will have nothing about them that is not beautiful. In the Chinese restaurant, where these navvies meet to have supper in the evening, I found them drinking tea out of china cups as delicate as the petals of a rose-leaf, whereas at the gaudy hotels I was supplied with a delf cup an inch and a half thick. When the Chinese bill was presented it was made out on rice paper, the account being done in Indian ink as fantastically as if an artist had been etching little birds on a fan.

Salt Lake City contains only two buildings of note, the chief being the Tabernacle, which is in the shape of a soup-kettle. It is decorated by the only native artist, and he has treated religious subjects in the naive spirit of the early Florentine painters, representing people of our own day in the dress of the period side by side with people of Biblical history who are clothed in some romantic costume.

The building next in importance is called the Amelia Palace, in honour of one of Brigham Young's wives. When he died the present president of the Mormons stood up in the Tabernacle and said that it had been revealed to him that he was to have the Amelia Palace, and that on this subject there were to be no more revelations of any kind!

From Salt Lake City one travels over the great plains of Colorado and up the Rocky Mountains, on the top of which is Leadville, the richest city in the world. It has also got the reputation of being the roughest, and every man carries a revolver. I was told that if I went there they would be sure to shoot me or my travelling manager. I wrote and told them that nothing that they could do to my travelling manager would intimidate me. They are miners—men working in metals, so I lectured to them on the Ethics of Art. I read them passages from the autobiography of Benvenuto Cellini and they seemed much delighted. I was reproved by my hearers for not having brought him with me. I explained that he had been dead for some little time which elicited the enquiry "Who shot him"? They afterwards took me to a dancing saloon where I saw the only rational method of art criticism I have ever come across. Over the piano was printed a notice:—

PLEASE DO NOT SHOOT THE PIANIST.

HE IS DOING HIS BEST.

The mortality among pianists in that place is marvellous. Then they asked me to supper, and having accepted, I had to descend a mine in a rickety bucket in which it was impossible to be graceful. Having got into the heart of the mountain I had supper, the first course being whisky, the second whisky and the third whisky.

I went to the Theatre to lecture and I was informed that just before I went there two men had been seized for committing a murder, and in that theatre they had been brought on to the stage at eight o'clock in the evening, and then and there tried and executed before a crowded audience. But I found these miners very charming and not at all rough.

Among the more elderly inhabitants of the South I found a melancholy tendency to date every event of importance by the late war. "How beautiful the moon is to-night," I once remarked to a gentleman who was standing next to me. "Yes," was his reply, "but you should have seen it before the war."

So infinitesimal did I find the knowledge of Art, west of the Rocky Mountains, that an art patron—one who in his day had been a miner—actually sued the railroad company for damages because the plaster cast of Venus of Milo, which he had imported from Paris, had been delivered minus the arms. And, what is more surprising still, he gained his case and the damages.

Pennsylvania, with its rocky gorges and woodland scenery, reminded me of Switzerland. The prairie reminded me of a piece of blotting-paper.

The Spanish and French have left behind them memorials in the beauty of their names. All the cities that have beautiful names derive them from the Spanish or the French. The English people give intensely ugly names to places. One place had such an ugly name that I refused to lecture there. It was called Grigsville. Supposing I had founded a school of Art there—fancy "Early Grigsville." Imagine a School of Art teaching "Grigsville Renaissance."

As for slang I did not hear much of it, though a young lady who had changed her clothes after an afternoon dance did say that "after the heel kick she shifted her day goods."

American youths are pale and precocious, or sallow and supercilious, but

American girls are pretty and charming—little oases of pretty unreasonableness in a vast desert of practical common-sense.

Every American girl is entitled to have twelve young men devoted to her. They remain her slaves and she rules them with charming nonchalance.

The men are entirely given to business; they have, as they say, their brains in front of their heads. They are also exceedingly acceptive of new ideas. Their education is practical. We base the education of children entirely on books, but we must give a child a mind before we can instruct the mind. Children have a natural antipathy to books—handicraft should be the basis of education. Boys and girls should be taught to use their hands to make something, and they would be less apt to destroy and be mischievous.

In going to America one learns that poverty is not a necessary accompaniment to civilisation. There at any rate is a country that has no trappings, no pageants and no gorgeous ceremonies. I saw only two processions—one was the Fire Brigade preceded by the Police, the other was the Police preceded by the Fire Brigade.

Every man when he gets to the age of twenty-one is allowed a vote, and thereby immediately acquires his political education. The Americans are the best politically educated people in the world. It is well worth one's while to go to a country which can teach us the beauty of the word FREEDOM and the value of the thing LIBERTY.

3. In a poem published in an American magazine on February 15th, 1882, Wilde wrote

"And in the throbbing engine room

Leap the long rods of polished steel."

4. Poems by Oscar Wilde. Also his Lecture on the English Renaissance. The Seaside Library, Vol. lviii. No. 1183, January 19th, 1882. 4to. Pp. 32. New York: George Munro, Publisher.

A copy of this edition was sold by auction in New York last year for eight dollars.

5. See An Essay concerning Human Understanding, IV. xii. 10.

A still more striking instance of the use of this expression is to be found in the same writer's Thoughts concerning Education, s. 28, where he says:—"Once in four and twenty hours, I think, is enough; and nobody, I guess, will think it too much."

OSCAR WILDE IN AMERICA.

An interesting account of Oscar Wilde, at the time of his American tour, was given in the Lady's Pictorial a few weeks after his arrival in New York, the city which he described as "one huge Whiteley's shop."

His Abode.

He was interviewed in a room which was intensely warm and the sofa on which the poet reclined was drawn up to the fire. An immense wolf rug, bordered with scarlet, was thrown over it and half-encircled his graceful form in its warm embrace. Wilde was wearied. In a languid, half enervated manner he gently sipped hot chocolate from a cup by his side. Occasionally he inhaled a long, deep whiff from a smouldering cigarette held lightly in his white and shapely hand.

His Dress.

He was attired in a smoking suit of dark brown velvet faced with lapels of red quilted silk. The ends of a long dark necktie floated over the facing like sea-weed on foam tinged by the dying sun. Dark brown nether garments, striped with red up the seam, and patent leather shoes with light cloth uppers completed the rest of the poet's costume.

His favourite colour is said to have been something between brown and green, a tint "that never was on sea or sky," and he had a complete suit made of it. A white walking-stick which he was in the habit of carrying was presented to him at the Acropolis and was said to have been cut from the olive groves of the Academia. Only in the evening was he wont to don knee breeches, "but evening and morning alike," adds his interviewer, "find him neither more nor less than a man, and always a perfect gentleman."

His appearance.

Long masses of dark brown hair, parted in the middle, fell in odd curves of beauty over his broad shoulders. He wore neither beard nor moustache.

The full, rather sensuous lips, now pressed close together with momentary tension, now parted in kindly smile, showed to perfection the nobility of his countenance.

A Grecian nose and a well-tinged flush of health on the poet's face added all that was required to make it a truly remarkable one. The eyes were large, dark[6] and ever-changing in expression. He was a charming companion who could tell racy stories and repeat bons mots of those whom society delighted to honour, and at the same time could cap quotations from Greek authors.

6. A French writer, M. Joseph-Renaud, recently described Wilde's eyes as being blue, while Lord Alfred Douglas affirms that they were green.

—

LADY WINDERMERE'S FAN

TO

THE DEAR MEMORY

OF

ROBERT EARL OF LYTTON

IN AFFECTION

AND

ADMIRATION

THE PERSONS OF THE PLAY

Lord Windermere

Lord Darlington

Lord Augustus Lorton

Mr. Dumby

Mr. Cecil Graham

Mr. Hopper

Parker, Butler

Lady Windermere

The Duchess of Berwick

Lady Agatha Carlisle

Lady Plymdale

Lady Stutfield

Lady Jedburgh

Mrs. Cowper-Cowper

Mrs. Erlynne

Rosalie, Maid

THE SCENES OF THE PLAY

ACT I.	*Morning-room in Lord Windermere's house.*
ACT II.	*Drawing-room in Lord Windermere's house.*
ACT III.	*Lord Darlington's rooms.*
ACT IV.	*Same as Act I.*
TIME:	*The Present.*
PLACE:	*London.*

The action of the play takes place within twenty-four hours, beginning on a Tuesday afternoon at five o'clock, and ending the next day at 1.30 p.m.

LONDON: ST. JAMES'S THEATRE

Lessee and Manager: Mr. George Alexander

February 22nd, 1892.

LORD WINDERMERE	*Mr. George Alexander.*
LORD DARLINGTON	*Mr. Nutcombe Gould.*
LORD AUGUSTUS LORTON	*Mr. H. H. Vincent.*
MR. CECIL GRAHAM	*Mr. Ben Webster.*
MR. DUMBY	*Mr. Vane-Tempest.*
MR. HOPPER	*Mr. Alfred Holles.*
PARKER (*Butler*)	*Mr. V. Sansbury.*
LADY WINDERMERE	*Miss Lily Hanbury.*
THE DUCHESS OF BERWICK	*Miss Fanny Coleman.*
LADY AGATHA CARLISLE	*Miss Laura Graves.*
LADY PLYMDALE	*Miss Granville.*
LADY JEDBURGH	*Miss B. Page.*
LADY STUTFIELD	*Miss Madge Girdlestone.*
MRS. COWPER-COWPER	*Miss A. de Winton.*
MRS. ERLYNNE	*Miss Marion Terry.*
ROSALIE (*Maid*)	*Miss Winifred Dolan.*

FIRST ACT

SCENE

Morning-room of Lord Windermere's house in Carlton House Terrace. Doors C. and R. Bureau with books and papers R. Sofa with small tea-table L. Window opening on to terrace L. Table R.

[Lady Windermere is at table R., arranging roses in a blue bowl.]

[Enter Parker.]

Parker. Is your ladyship at home this afternoon?

Lady Windermere. Yes—who has called?

Parker. Lord Darlington, my lady.

Lady Windermere. [Hesitates for a moment.] Show him up—and I'm at home to any one who calls.

Parker. Yes, my lady.

[Exit C.]

Lady Windermere. It's best for me to see him before to-night. I'm glad he's come.

[Enter Parker C.]

Parker. Lord Darlington,

[Enter Lord Darlington C.]

[Exit Parker.]

Lord Darlington. How do you do, Lady Windermere?

Lady Windermere. How do you do, Lord Darlington? No, I can't shake hands with you. My hands are all wet with these roses. Aren't they lovely? They came up from Selby this morning.

Lord Darlington. They are quite perfect. [Sees a fan lying on the table.] And what a wonderful fan! May I look at it?

Lady Windermere. Do. Pretty, isn't it! It's got my name on it, and everything. I have only just seen it myself. It's my husband's birthday present to me. You know to-day is my birthday?

Lord Darlington. No? Is it really?

Lady Windermere. Yes, I'm of age to-day. Quite an important day in my life, isn't it? That is why I am giving this party to-night. Do sit down. [Still arranging flowers.]

Lord Darlington. [Sitting down.] I wish I had known it was your birthday, Lady Windermere. I would have covered the whole street in front of your house with flowers for you to walk on. They are made for you.

[A short pause.]

Lady Windermere. Lord Darlington, you annoyed me last night at the Foreign Office. I am afraid you are going to annoy me again.

Lord Darlington. I, Lady Windermere?

[Enter Parker and Footman C., with tray and tea things.]

Lady Windermere. Put it there, Parker. That will do. [Wipes her hands with her pocket-handkerchief, goes to tea-table, and sits down.] Won't you come over, Lord Darlington?

[Exit Parker C.]

Lord Darlington. [Takes chair and goes across L.C.] I am quite miserable, Lady Windermere. You must tell me what I did. [Sits down at table L.]

Lady Windermere. Well, you kept paying me elaborate compliments the whole evening.

Lord Darlington. [Smiling.] Ah, nowadays we are all of us so hard up, that the only pleasant things to pay are compliments. They're the only things we can pay.

40

Lady Windermere. [Shaking her head.] No, I am talking very seriously. You mustn't laugh, I am quite serious. I don't like compliments, and I don't see why a man should think he is pleasing a woman enormously when he says to her a whole heap of things that he doesn't mean.

Lord Darlington. Ah, but I did mean them. [Takes tea which she offers him.]

Lady Windermere. [Gravely.] I hope not. I should be sorry to have to quarrel with you, Lord Darlington. I like you very much, you know that. But I shouldn't like you at all if I thought you were what most other men are. Believe me, you are better than most other men, and I sometimes think you pretend to be worse.

Lord Darlington. We all have our little vanities, Lady Windermere.

Lady Windermere. Why do you make that your special one? [Still seated at table L.]

Lord Darlington. [Still seated L.C.] Oh, nowadays so many conceited people go about Society pretending to be good, that I think it shows rather a sweet and modest disposition to pretend to be bad. Besides, there is this to be said. If you pretend to be good, the world takes you very seriously. If you pretend to be bad, it doesn't. Such is the astounding stupidity of optimism.

Lady Windermere. Don't you want the world to take you seriously then, Lord Darlington?

Lord Darlington. No, not the world. Who are the people the world takes seriously? All the dull people one can think of, from the Bishops down to the bores. I should like you to take me very seriously, Lady Windermere, you more than any one else in life.

Lady Windermere. Why—why me?

Lord Darlington. [After a slight hesitation.] Because I think we might be great friends. Let us be great friends. You may want a friend some day.

Lady Windermere. Why do you say that?

Lord Darlington. Oh!—we all want friends at times.

Lady Windermere. I think we're very good friends already, Lord Darlington. We can always remain so as long as you don't—

Lord Darlington. Don't what?

Lady Windermere. Don't spoil it by saying extravagant silly things to me. You think I am a Puritan, I suppose? Well, I have something of the Puritan in me. I was brought up like that. I am glad of it. My mother died when I was a mere child. I lived always with Lady Julia, my father's elder sister, you know. She was stern to me, but she taught me what the world is forgetting, the difference that there is between what is right and what is wrong. She allowed of no compromise. I allow of none.

Lord Darlington. My dear Lady Windermere!

Lady Windermere. [Leaning back on the sofa.] You look on me as being behind the age.—Well, I am! I should be sorry to be on the same level as an age like this.

Lord Darlington. You think the age very bad?

Lady Windermere. Yes. Nowadays people seem to look on life as a speculation. It is not a speculation. It is a sacrament. Its ideal is Love. Its purification is sacrifice.

Lord Darlington. [Smiling.] Oh, anything is better than being sacrificed!

Lady Windermere. [Leaning forward.] Don't say that.

Lord Darlington. I do say it. I feel it—I know it.

[Enter Parker C.]

Parker. The men want to know if they are to put the carpets on the terrace for to-night, my lady?

Lady Windermere. You don't think it will rain, Lord Darlington, do you?

Lord Darlington. I won't hear of its raining on your birthday!

Lady Windermere. Tell them to do it at once, Parker.

[Exit Parker C.]

Lord Darlington. [Still seated.] Do you think then—of course I am only putting an imaginary instance—do you think that in the case of a young married couple, say about two years married, if the husband suddenly becomes the intimate friend of a woman of—well, more than doubtful character—is always calling upon her, lunching with her, and probably paying her bills—do you think that the wife should not console herself?

Lady Windermere. [Frowning.] Console herself?

Lord Darlington. Yes, I think she should—I think she has the right.

Lady Windermere. Because the husband is vile—should the wife be vile also?

Lord Darlington. Vileness is a terrible word, Lady Windermere.

Lady Windermere. It is a terrible thing, Lord Darlington.

Lord Darlington. Do you know I am afraid that good people do a great deal of harm in this world. Certainly the greatest harm they do is that they make badness of such extraordinary importance. It is absurd to divide people into good and bad. People are either charming or tedious. I take the side of the charming, and you, Lady Windermere, can't help belonging to them.

Lady Windermere. Now, Lord Darlington. [Rising and crossing R., front of him.] Don't stir, I am merely going to finish my flowers. [Goes to table R.C.]

Lord Darlington. [Rising and moving chair.] And I must say I think you are very hard on modern life, Lady Windermere. Of course there is much against it, I admit. Most women, for instance, nowadays, are rather mercenary.

Lady Windermere. Don't talk about such people.

Lord Darlington. Well then, setting aside mercenary people, who, of

43

course, are dreadful, do you think seriously that women who have committed what the world calls a fault should never be forgiven?

Lady Windermere. [Standing at table.] I think they should never be forgiven.

Lord Darlington. And men? Do you think that there should be the same laws for men as there are for women?

Lady Windermere. Certainly!

Lord Darlington. I think life too complex a thing to be settled by these hard and fast rules.

Lady Windermere. If we had 'these hard and fast rules,' we should find life much more simple.

Lord Darlington. You allow of no exceptions?

Lady Windermere. None!

Lord Darlington. Ah, what a fascinating Puritan you are, Lady Windermere!

Lady Windermere. The adjective was unnecessary, Lord Darlington.

Lord Darlington. I couldn't help it. I can resist everything except temptation.

Lady Windermere. You have the modern affectation of weakness.

Lord Darlington. [Looking at her.] It's only an affectation, Lady Windermere.

[Enter Parker C.]

Parker. The Duchess of Berwick and Lady Agatha Carlisle.

[Enter the Duchess of Berwick and Lady Agatha Carlisle C.]

[Exit Parker C.]

Duchess of Berwick. [Coming down C., and shaking hands.] Dear

Margaret, I am so pleased to see you. You remember Agatha, don't you? [Crossing L.C.] How do you do, Lord Darlington? I won't let you know my daughter, you are far too wicked.

Lord Darlington. Don't say that, Duchess. As a wicked man I am a complete failure. Why, there are lots of people who say I have never really done anything wrong in the whole course of my life. Of course they only say it behind my back.

Duchess of Berwick. Isn't he dreadful? Agatha, this is Lord Darlington. Mind you don't believe a word he says. [Lord Darlington crosses R.C.] No, no tea, thank you, dear. [Crosses and sits on sofa.] We have just had tea at Lady Markby's. Such bad tea, too. It was quite undrinkable. I wasn't at all surprised. Her own son-in-law supplies it. Agatha is looking forward so much to your ball to-night, dear Margaret.

Lady Windermere. [Seated L.C.] Oh, you mustn't think it is going to be a ball, Duchess. It is only a dance in honour of my birthday. A small and early.

Lord Darlington. [Standing L.C.] Very small, very early, and very select, Duchess.

Duchess of Berwick. [On sofa L.] Of course it's going to be select. But we know that, dear Margaret, about your house. It is really one of the few houses in London where I can take Agatha, and where I feel perfectly secure about dear Berwick. I don't know what society is coming to. The most dreadful people seem to go everywhere. They certainly come to my parties— the men get quite furious if one doesn't ask them. Really, some one should make a stand against it.

Lady Windermere. I will, Duchess. I will have no one in my house about whom there is any scandal.

Lord Darlington. [R.C.] Oh, don't say that, Lady Windermere. I should never be admitted! [Sitting.]

Duchess of Berwick. Oh, men don't matter. With women it is different.

We're good. Some of us are, at least. But we are positively getting elbowed into the corner. Our husbands would really forget our existence if we didn't nag at them from time to time, just to remind them that we have a perfect legal right to do so.

Lord Darlington.   It's a curious thing, Duchess, about the game of marriage—a game, by the way, that is going out of fashion—the wives hold all the honours, and invariably lose the odd trick.

Duchess of Berwick.   The odd trick?   Is that the husband, Lord Darlington?

Lord Darlington.   It would be rather a good name for the modern husband.

Duchess of Berwick.   Dear Lord Darlington, how thoroughly depraved you are!

Lady Windermere.   Lord Darlington is trivial.

Lord Darlington.   Ah, don't say that, Lady Windermere.

Lady Windermere.   Why do you talk so trivially about life, then?

Lord Darlington.   Because I think that life is far too important a thing ever to talk seriously about it. [Moves up C.]

Duchess of Berwick.   What does he mean?   Do, as a concession to my poor wits, Lord Darlington, just explain to me what you really mean.

Lord Darlington.   [Coming down back of table.]   I think I had better not, Duchess.   Nowadays to be intelligible is to be found out.   Good-bye! [Shakes hands with Duchess.] And now—[goes up stage] Lady Windermere, good-bye. I may come to-night, mayn't I? Do let me come.

Lady Windermere.   [Standing up stage with Lord Darlington.]   Yes, certainly.   But you are not to say foolish, insincere things to people.

Lord Darlington.   [Smiling.] Ah! you are beginning to reform me. It is a dangerous thing to reform any one, Lady Windermere. [Bows, and exit C.]

Duchess of Berwick. [Who has risen, goes C.] What a charming, wicked creature! I like him so much. I'm quite delighted he's gone! How sweet you're looking! Where do you get your gowns? And now I must tell you how sorry I am for you, dear Margaret. [Crosses to sofa and sits with Lady Windermere.] Agatha, darling!

Lady Agatha. Yes, mamma. [Rises.]

Duchess of Berwick. Will you go and look over the photograph album that I see there?

Lady Agatha. Yes, mamma. [Goes to table up L.]

Duchess of Berwick. Dear girl! She is so fond of photographs of Switzerland. Such a pure taste, I think. But I really am so sorry for you, Margaret.

Lady Windermere. [Smiling.] Why, Duchess?

Duchess of Berwick. Oh, on account of that horrid woman. She dresses so well, too, which makes it much worse, sets such a dreadful example. Augustus—you know my disreputable brother—such a trial to us all—well, Augustus is completely infatuated about her. It is quite scandalous, for she is absolutely inadmissible into society. Many a woman has a past, but I am told that she has at least a dozen, and that they all fit.

Lady Windermere. Whom are you talking about, Duchess?

Duchess of Berwick. About Mrs. Erlynne.

Lady Windermere. Mrs. Erlynne? I never heard of her, Duchess. And what has she to do with me?

Duchess of Berwick. My poor child! Agatha, darling!

Lady Agatha. Yes, mamma.

Duchess of Berwick. Will you go out on the terrace and look at the sunset?

Lady Agatha. Yes, mamma.

[Exit through window, L.]

Duchess of Berwick. Sweet girl! So devoted to sunsets! Shows such refinement of feeling, does it not? After all, there is nothing like Nature, is there?

Lady Windermere. But what is it, Duchess? Why do you talk to me about this person?

Duchess of Berwick. Don't you really know? I assure you we're all so distressed about it. Only last night at dear Lady Jansen's every one was saying how extraordinary it was that, of all men in London, Windermere should behave in such a way.

Lady Windermere. My husband—what has he got to do with any woman of that kind?

Duchess of Berwick. Ah, what indeed, dear? That is the point. He goes to see her continually, and stops for hours at a time, and while he is there she is not at home to any one. Not that many ladies call on her, dear, but she has a great many disreputable men friends—my own brother particularly, as I told you—and that is what makes it so dreadful about Windermere. We looked upon him as being such a model husband, but I am afraid there is no doubt about it. My dear nieces—you know the Saville girls, don't you?—such nice domestic creatures—plain, dreadfully plain, but so good—well, they're always at the window doing fancy work, and making ugly things for the poor, which I think so useful of them in these dreadful socialistic days, and this terrible woman has taken a house in Curzon Street, right opposite them—such a respectable street, too! I don't know what we're coming to! And they tell me that Windermere goes there four and five times a week—they see him. They can't help it—and although they never talk scandal, they—well, of course—they remark on it to every one. And the worst of it all is that I have been told that this woman has got a great deal of money out of somebody, for it seems that she came to London six months ago without anything at all to speak of, and now she has this charming house in Mayfair, drives her ponies in the Park every afternoon and all—well, all—since she has known poor dear Windermere.

Lady Windermere. Oh, I can't believe it!

Duchess of Berwick. But it's quite true, my dear. The whole of London knows it. That is why I felt it was better to come and talk to you, and advise you to take Windermere away at once to Homburg or to Aix, where he'll have something to amuse him, and where you can watch him all day long. I assure you, my dear, that on several occasions after I was first married, I had to pretend to be very ill, and was obliged to drink the most unpleasant mineral waters, merely to get Berwick out of town. He was so extremely susceptible. Though I am bound to say he never gave away any large sums of money to anybody. He is far too high-principled for that!

Lady Windermere. [Interrupting.] Duchess, Duchess, it's impossible! [Rising and crossing stage to C.] We are only married two years. Our child is but six months old. [Sits in chair R. of L. table.]

Duchess of Berwick. Ah, the dear pretty baby! How is the little darling? Is it a boy or a girl? I hope a girl—Ah, no, I remember it's a boy! I'm so sorry. Boys are so wicked. My boy is excessively immoral. You wouldn't believe at what hours he comes home. And he's only left Oxford a few months—I really don't know what they teach them there.

Lady Windermere. Are all men bad?

Duchess of Berwick. Oh, all of them, my dear, all of them, without any exception. And they never grow any better. Men become old, but they never become good.

Lady Windermere. Windermere and I married for love.

Duchess of Berwick. Yes, we begin like that. It was only Berwick's brutal and incessant threats of suicide that made me accept him at all, and before the year was out, he was running after all kinds of petticoats, every colour, every shape, every material. In fact, before the honeymoon was over, I caught him winking at my maid, a most pretty, respectable girl. I dismissed her at once without a character.—No, I remember I passed her on to my sister; poor dear Sir George is so short-sighted, I thought it wouldn't matter. But it did, though—it was most unfortunate. [Rises.] And now, my dear child, I must go, as we are dining out. And mind you don't take this little aberration of Windermere's too much to heart. Just take him abroad, and he'll come back to you all right.

Lady Windermere. Come back to me? [C.]

Duchess of Berwick. [L.C.] Yes, dear, these wicked women get our husbands away from us, but they always come back, slightly damaged, of course. And don't make scenes, men hate them!

Lady Windermere. It is very kind of you, Duchess, to come and tell me all this. But I can't believe that my husband is untrue to me.

Duchess of Berwick. Pretty child! I was like that once. Now I know that all men are monsters. [Lady Windermere rings bell.] The only thing to do is to feed the wretches well. A good cook does wonders, and that I know you have. My dear Margaret, you are not going to cry?

Lady Windermere. You needn't be afraid, Duchess, I never cry.

Duchess of Berwick. That's quite right, dear. Crying is the refuge of plain women but the ruin of pretty ones. Agatha, darling!

Lady Agatha. [Entering L.] Yes, mamma. [Stands back of table L.C.]

Duchess of Berwick. Come and bid good-bye to Lady Windermere, and thank her for your charming visit. [Coming down again.] And by the way, I must thank you for sending a card to Mr. Hopper—he's that rich young Australian people are taking such notice of just at present. His father made a great fortune by selling some kind of food in circular tins—most palatable, I believe—I fancy it is the thing the servants always refuse to eat. But the son is quite interesting. I think he's attracted by dear Agatha's clever talk. Of course, we should be very sorry to lose her, but I think that a mother who doesn't part with a daughter every season has no real affection. We're coming to-night, dear. [Parker opens C. doors.] And remember my advice, take the poor fellow out of town at once, it is the only thing to do. Good-bye, once more; come, Agatha.

[Exeunt Duchess and Lady Agatha C.]

Lady Windermere. How horrible! I understand now what Lord Darlington meant by the imaginary instance of the couple not two years married. Oh! it can't be true—she spoke of enormous sums of money paid to this woman. I know where Arthur keeps his bank book—in one of the drawers of that desk. I might find out by that. I will find out. [Opens drawer.] No, it is some hideous mistake. [Rises and goes C.] Some silly scandal! He loves me! He loves me! But why should I not look? I am his wife, I have a right to look! [Returns to bureau, takes out book and examines it page by page, smiles and gives a sigh of relief.] I knew it! there is not a word of truth in this stupid story. [Puts book back in drawer. As he does so, starts and takes out another book.] A second book—private—locked! [Tries to open it, but fails. Sees paper knife on bureau, and with it cuts cover from book. Begins to start at the first page.] 'Mrs. Erlynne—£600—Mrs. Erlynne—£700—Mrs. Erlynne—£400.' Oh! it is true! It is true! How horrible! [Throws book on floor.]

[Enter Lord Windermere C.]

Lord Windermere. Well, dear, has the fan been sent home yet? [Going R.C. Sees book.] Margaret, you have cut open my bank book. You have no right to do such a thing!

Lady Windermere. You think it wrong that you are found out, don't you?

Lord Windermere. I think it wrong that a wife should spy on her husband.

Lady Windermere. I did not spy on you. I never knew of this woman's existence till half an hour ago. Some one who pitied me was kind enough to tell me what every one in London knows already—your daily visits to Curzon Street, your mad infatuation, the monstrous sums of money you squander on this infamous woman! [Crossing L.]

Lord Windermere. Margaret! don't talk like that of Mrs. Erlynne, you don't know how unjust it is!

Lady Windermere. [Turning to him.] You are very jealous of Mrs.

Erlynne's honour. I wish you had been as jealous of mine.

Lord Windermere. Your honour is untouched, Margaret. You don't think for a moment that—[Puts book back into desk.]

Lady Windermere. I think that you spend your money strangely. That is all. Oh, don't imagine I mind about the money. As far as I am concerned, you may squander everything we have. But what I do mind is that you who have loved me, you who have taught me to love you, should pass from the love that is given to the love that is bought. Oh, it's horrible! [Sits on sofa.] And it is I who feel degraded! you don't feel anything. I feel stained, utterly stained. You can't realise how hideous the last six months seems to me now—every kiss you have given me is tainted in my memory.

Lord Windermere. [Crossing to her.] Don't say that, Margaret. I never loved any one in the whole world but you.

Lady Windermere. [Rises.] Who is this woman, then? Why do you take a house for her?

Lord Windermere. I did not take a house for her.

Lady Windermere. You gave her the money to do it, which is the same thing.

Lord Windermere. Margaret, as far as I have known Mrs. Erlynne—

Lady Windermere. Is there a Mr. Erlynne—or is he a myth?

Lord Windermere. Her husband died many years ago. She is alone in the world.

Lady Windermere. No relations? [A pause.]

Lord Windermere. None.

Lady Windermere. Rather curious, isn't it? [L.]

Lord Windermere. [L.C.] Margaret, I was saying to you—and I beg you to listen to me—that as far as I have known Mrs. Erlynne, she has conducted herself well. If years ago—

Lady Windermere. Oh! [Crossing R.C.] I don't want details about her life!

Lord Windermere. [C.] I am not going to give you any details about her life. I tell you simply this—Mrs. Erlynne was once honoured, loved, respected. She was well born, she had position—she lost everything—threw it away, if you like. That makes it all the more bitter. Misfortunes one can endure—they come from outside, they are accidents. But to suffer for one's own faults—ah!—there is the sting of life. It was twenty years ago, too. She was little more than a girl then. She had been a wife for even less time than you have.

Lady Windermere. I am not interested in her—and—you should not mention this woman and me in the same breath. It is an error of taste. [Sitting R. at desk.]

Lord Windermere. Margaret, you could save this woman. She wants to get back into society, and she wants you to help her. [Crossing to her.]

Lady Windermere. Me!

Lord Windermere. Yes, you.

Lady Windermere. How impertinent of her! [A pause.]

Lord Windermere. Margaret, I came to ask you a great favour, and I still ask it of you, though you have discovered what I had intended you should never have known that I have given Mrs. Erlynne a large sum of money. I want you to send her an invitation for our party to-night. [Standing L. of her.]

Lady Windermere. You are mad! [Rises.]

Lord Windermere. I entreat you. People may chatter about her, do chatter about her, of course, but they don't know anything definite against her. She has been to several houses—not to houses where you would go, I admit, but still to houses where women who are in what is called Society nowadays do go. That does not content her. She wants you to receive her once.

Lady Windermere. As a triumph for her, I suppose?

Lord Windermere. No; but because she knows that you are a good woman—and that if she comes here once she will have a chance of a happier, a surer life than she has had. She will make no further effort to know you. Won't you help a woman who is trying to get back?

Lady Windermere. No! If a woman really repents, she never wishes to return to the society that has made or seen her ruin.

Lord Windermere. I beg of you.

Lady Windermere. [Crossing to door R.] I am going to dress for dinner, and don't mention the subject again this evening. Arthur [going to him C.], you fancy because I have no father or mother that I am alone in the world, and that you can treat me as you choose. You are wrong, I have friends, many friends.

Lord Windermere. [L.C.] Margaret, you are talking foolishly, recklessly. I won't argue with you, but I insist upon your asking Mrs. Erlynne to-night.

Lady Windermere. [R.C.] I shall do nothing of the kind. [Crossing L.C.]

Lord Windermere. You refuse? [C.]

Lady Windermere. Absolutely!

Lord Windermere. Ah, Margaret, do this for my sake; it is her last chance.

Lady Windermere. What has that to do with me?

Lord Windermere. How hard good women are!

Lady Windermere. How weak bad men are!

Lord Windermere. Margaret, none of us men may be good enough for the women we marry—that is quite true—but you don't imagine I would ever—oh, the suggestion is monstrous!

Lady Windermere. Why should you be different from other men? I am told that there is hardly a husband in London who does not waste his life over some shameful passion.

Lord Windermere. I am not one of them.

Lady Windermere. I am not sure of that!

Lord Windermere. You are sure in your heart. But don't make chasm after chasm between us. God knows the last few minutes have thrust us wide enough apart. Sit down and write the card.

Lady Windermere. Nothing in the whole world would induce me.

Lord Windermere. [Crossing to bureau.] Then I will! [Rings electric bell, sits and writes card.]

Lady Windermere. You are going to invite this woman? [Crossing to him.]

Lord Windermere. Yes. [Pause. Enter Parker.] Parker!

Parker. Yes, my lord. [Comes down L.C.]

Lord Windermere. Have this note sent to Mrs. Erlynne at No. 84A Curzon Street. [Crossing to L.C. and giving note to Parker.] There is no answer!

[Exit Parker C.]

Lady Windermere. Arthur, if that woman comes here, I shall insult her.

Lord Windermere. Margaret, don't say that.

Lady Windermere. I mean it.

Lord Windermere. Child, if you did such a thing, there's not a woman in London who wouldn't pity you.

Lady Windermere. There is not a good woman in London who would not applaud me. We have been too lax. We must make an example. I propose to begin to-night. [Picking up fan.] Yes, you gave me this fan to-day; it was your birthday present. If that woman crosses my threshold, I shall strike her across the face with it.

Lord Windermere. Margaret, you couldn't do such a thing.

Lady Windermere. You don't know me! [Moves R.]

[Enter Parker.]

Parker!

Parker. Yes, my lady.

Lady Windermere. I shall dine in my own room. I don't want dinner, in fact. See that everything is ready by half-past ten. And, Parker, be sure you pronounce the names of the guests very distinctly to-night. Sometimes you speak so fast that I miss them. I am particularly anxious to hear the names quite clearly, so as to make no mistake. You understand, Parker?

Parker. Yes, my lady.

Lady Windermere. That will do!

[Exit Parker C.]

[Speaking to Lord Windermere.] Arthur, if that woman comes here—I warn you—

Lord Windermere. Margaret, you'll ruin us!

Lady Windermere. Us! From this moment my life is separate from yours. But if you wish to avoid a public scandal, write at once to this woman, and tell her that I forbid her to come here!

Lord Windermere. I will not—I cannot—she must come!

Lady Windermere. Then I shall do exactly as I have said. [Goes R.] You leave me no choice.

[Exit R.]

Lord Windermere. [Calling after her.] Margaret! Margaret! [A pause.] My God! What shall I do? I dare not tell her who this woman really is. The shame would kill her. [Sinks down into a chair and buries his face in his hands.]

ACT DROP

SECOND ACT

SCENE

Drawing-room in Lord Windermere's house. Door R.U. opening into ball-room, where band is playing. Door L. through which guests are entering. Door L.U. opens on to illuminated terrace. Palms, flowers, and brilliant lights. Room crowded with guests. Lady Windermere is receiving them.

Duchess of Berwick. [Up C.] So strange Lord Windermere isn't here. Mr. Hopper is very late, too. You have kept those five dances for him, Agatha? [Comes down.]

Lady Agatha. Yes, mamma.

Duchess of Berwick. [Sitting on sofa.] Just let me see your card. I'm so glad Lady Windermere has revived cards.—They're a mother's only safeguard. You dear simple little thing! [Scratches out two names.] No nice girl should ever waltz with such particularly younger sons! It looks so fast! The last two dances you might pass on the terrace with Mr. Hopper.

[Enter Mr. Dumby and Lady Plymdale from the ball-room.]

Lady Agatha. Yes, mamma.

Duchess of Berwick. [Fanning herself.] The air is so pleasant there.

Parker. Mrs. Cowper-Cowper. Lady Stutfield. Sir James Royston. Mr. Guy Berkeley.

[These people enter as announced.]

Dumby. Good evening, Lady Stutfield. I suppose this will be the last ball of the season?

Lady Stutfield. I suppose so, Mr. Dumby. It's been a delightful season, hasn't it?

Dumby. Quite delightful! Good evening, Duchess. I suppose this will be the last ball of the season?

Duchess of Berwick. I suppose so, Mr. Dumby. It has been a very dull season, hasn't it?

Dumby. Dreadfully dull! Dreadfully dull!

Mr. Cowper-Cowper. Good evening, Mr. Dumby. I suppose this will be the last ball of the season?

Dumby. Oh, I think not. There'll probably be two more. [Wanders back to Lady Plymdale.]

Parker. Mr. Rufford. Lady Jedburgh and Miss Graham. Mr. Hopper.

[These people enter as announced.]

Hopper. How do you do, Lady Windermere? How do you do, Duchess? [Bows to Lady Agatha.]

Duchess of Berwick. Dear Mr. Hopper, how nice of you to come so early. We all know how you are run after in London.

Hopper. Capital place, London! They are not nearly so exclusive in London as they are in Sydney.

Duchess of Berwick. Ah! we know your value, Mr. Hopper. We wish there were more like you. It would make life so much easier. Do you know, Mr. Hopper, dear Agatha and I are so much interested in Australia. It must be so pretty with all the dear little kangaroos flying about. Agatha has found it on the map. What a curious shape it is! Just like a large packing case. However, it is a very young country, isn't it?

Hopper. Wasn't it made at the same time as the others, Duchess?

Duchess of Berwick. How clever you are, Mr. Hopper. You have a cleverness quite of your own. Now I mustn't keep you.

Hopper. But I should like to dance with Lady Agatha, Duchess.

Duchess of Berwick. Well, I hope she has a dance left. Have you a dance left, Agatha?

Lady Agatha. Yes, mamma.

Duchess of Berwick. The next one?

Lady Agatha. Yes, mamma.

Hopper. May I have the pleasure? [Lady Agatha bows.]

Duchess of Berwick. Mind you take great care of my little chatterbox, Mr. Hopper.

[Lady Agatha and Mr. Hopper pass into ball-room.]

[Enter Lord Windermere.]

Lord Windermere. Margaret, I want to speak to you.

Lady Windermere. In a moment. [The music drops.]

Parker. Lord Augustus Lorton.

[Enter Lord Augustus.]

Lord Augustus. Good evening, Lady Windermere.

Duchess of Berwick. Sir James, will you take me into the ball-room? Augustus has been dining with us to-night. I really have had quite enough of dear Augustus for the moment.

[Sir James Royston gives the Duchess his aim and escorts her into the ball-room.]

Parker. Mr. and Mrs. Arthur Bowden. Lord and Lady Paisley. Lord Darlington.

[These people enter as announced.]

Lord Augustus. [Coming up to Lord Windermere.] Want to speak to you particularly, dear boy. I'm worn to a shadow. Know I don't look it. None of us men do look what we really are. Demmed good thing, too. What I want to know is this. Who is she? Where does she come from? Why hasn't she got any demmed relations? Demmed nuisance, relations! But they make one so demmed respectable.

Lord Windermere. You are talking of Mrs. Erlynne, I suppose? I only met her six months ago. Till then, I never knew of her existence.

Lord Augustus. You have seen a good deal of her since then.

Lord Windermere. [Coldly.] Yes, I have seen a good deal of her since then. I have just seen her.

Lord Augustus. Egad! the women are very down on her. I have been dining with Arabella this evening! By Jove! you should have heard what she said about Mrs. Erlynne. She didn't leave a rag on her. . . . [Aside.] Berwick and I told her that didn't matter much, as the lady in question must have an extremely fine figure. You should have seen Arabella's expression! . . . But, look here, dear boy. I don't know what to do about Mrs. Erlynne. Egad! I might be married to her; she treats me with such demmed indifference. She's deuced clever, too! She explains everything. Egad! she explains you. She has got any amount of explanations for you—and all of them different.

Lord Windermere. No explanations are necessary about my friendship with Mrs. Erlynne.

Lord Augustus. Hem! Well, look here, dear old fellow. Do you think she will ever get into this demmed thing called Society? Would you introduce her to your wife? No use beating about the confounded bush. Would you do that?

Lord Windermere. Mrs. Erlynne is coming here to-night.

Lord Augustus. Your wife has sent her a card?

Lord Windermere. Mrs. Erlynne has received a card.

Lord Augustus. Then she's all right, dear boy. But why didn't you tell me that before? It would have saved me a heap of worry and demmed misunderstandings!

[Lady Agatha and Mr. Hopper cross and exit on terrace L.U.E.]

Parker. Mr. Cecil Graham!

[Enter Mr. Cecil Graham.]

Cecil Graham. [Bows to Lady Windermere, passes over and shakes hands with Lord Windermere.] Good evening, Arthur. Why don't you ask me how I am? I like people to ask me how I am. It shows a wide-spread interest in my health. Now, to-night I am not at all well. Been dining with my people. Wonder why it is one's people are always so tedious? My father would talk morality after dinner. I told him he was old enough to know better. But my experience is that as soon as people are old enough to know better, they don't know anything at all. Hallo, Tuppy! Hear you're going to be married again; thought you were tired of that game.

Lord Augustus. You're excessively trivial, my dear boy, excessively trivial!

Cecil Graham. By the way, Tuppy, which is it? Have you been twice married and once divorced, or twice divorced and once married? I say you've been twice divorced and once married. It seems so much more probable.

Lord Augustus. I have a very bad memory. I really don't remember which. [Moves away R.]

Lady Plymdale. Lord Windermere, I've something most particular to ask you.

Lord Windermere. I am afraid—if you will excuse me—I must join my wife.

Lady Plymdale. Oh, you mustn't dream of such a thing. It's most dangerous nowadays for a husband to pay any attention to his wife in public. It always makes people think that he beats her when they're alone. The world has grown so suspicious of anything that looks like a happy married life. But I'll tell you what it is at supper. [Moves towards door of ball-room.]

Lord Windermere. [C.] Margaret! I must speak to you.

Lady Windermere. Will you hold my fan for me, Lord Darlington? Thanks. [Comes down to him.]

Lord Windermere. [Crossing to her.] Margaret, what you said before dinner was, of course, impossible?

Lady Windermere. That woman is not coming here to-night!

Lord Windermere. [R.C.] Mrs. Erlynne is coming here, and if you in any way annoy or wound her, you will bring shame and sorrow on us both. Remember that! Ah, Margaret! only trust me! A wife should trust her husband!

Lady Windermere. [C.] London is full of women who trust their husbands. One can always recognise them. They look so thoroughly unhappy. I am not going to be one of them. [Moves up.] Lord Darlington, will you give me back my fan, please? Thanks. . . . A useful thing a fan, isn't it? . . . I want a friend to-night, Lord Darlington: I didn't know I would want one so soon.

Lord Darlington. Lady Windermere! I knew the time would come some day; but why to-night?

Lord Windermere. I will tell her. I must. It would be terrible if there were any scene. Margaret . . .

Parker. Mrs. Erlynne!

[Lord Windermere starts. Mrs. Erlynne enters, very beautifully dressed and very dignified. Lady Windermere clutches at her fan, then lets it drop on the door. She bows coldly to Mrs. Erlynne, who bows to her sweetly in turn, and sails into the room.]

Lord Darlington. You have dropped your fan, Lady Windermere. [Picks it up and hands it to her.]

Mrs. Erlynne. [C.] How do you do, again, Lord Windermere? How charming your sweet wife looks! Quite a picture!

Lord Windermere. [In a low voice.] It was terribly rash of you to come!

Mrs. Erlynne. [Smiling.] The wisest thing I ever did in my life. And, by the way, you must pay me a good deal of attention this evening. I am afraid of the women. You must introduce me to some of them. The men I can always manage. How do you do, Lord Augustus? You have quite neglected me lately. I have not seen you since yesterday. I am afraid you're faithless. Every one told me so.

Lord Augustus. [R.] Now really, Mrs. Erlynne, allow me to explain.

Mrs. Erlynne. [R.C.] No, dear Lord Augustus, you can't explain anything. It is your chief charm.

Lord Augustus. Ah! if you find charms in me, Mrs. Erlynne—

[They converse together. Lord Windermere moves uneasily about the room watching Mrs. Erlynne.]

Lord Darlington. [To Lady Windermere.] How pale you are!

Lady Windermere. Cowards are always pale!

Lord Darlington. You look faint. Come out on the terrace.

Lady Windermere. Yes. [To Parker.] Parker, send my cloak out.

Mrs. Erlynne. [Crossing to her.] Lady Windermere, how beautifully your terrace is illuminated. Reminds me of Prince Doria's at Rome.

[Lady Windermere bows coldly, and goes off with Lord Darlington.]

Oh, how do you do, Mr. Graham? Isn't that your aunt, Lady Jedburgh? I should so much like to know her.

Cecil Graham. [After a moment's hesitation and embarrassment.] Oh, certainly, if you wish it. Aunt Caroline, allow me to introduce Mrs. Erlynne.

Mrs. Erlynne. So pleased to meet you, Lady Jedburgh. [Sits beside her on the sofa.] Your nephew and I are great friends. I am so much interested in his political career. I think he's sure to be a wonderful success. He thinks like a Tory, and talks like a Radical, and that's so important nowadays. He's such a brilliant talker, too. But we all know from whom he inherits that. Lord Allandale was saying to me only yesterday, in the Park, that Mr. Graham talks almost as well as his aunt.

Lady Jedburgh. [R.] Most kind of you to say these charming things to me! [Mrs. Erlynne smiles, and continues conversation.]

Dumby. [To Cecil Graham.] Did you introduce Mrs. Erlynne to Lady Jedburgh?

Cecil Graham. Had to, my dear fellow. Couldn't help it! That woman can make one do anything she wants. How, I don't know.

Dumby. Hope to goodness she won't speak to me! [Saunters towards Lady Plymdale.]

Mrs. Erlynne. [C. To Lady Jedburgh.] On Thursday? With great pleasure. [Rises, and speaks to Lord Windermere, laughing.] What a bore it is to have to be civil to these old dowagers! But they always insist on it!

Lady Plymdale. [To Mr. Dumby.] Who is that well-dressed woman talking to Windermere?

Dumby. Haven't got the slightest idea! Looks like an édition de luxe of a wicked French novel, meant specially for the English market.

Mrs. Erlynne. So that is poor Dumby with Lady Plymdale? I hear she is frightfully jealous of him. He doesn't seem anxious to speak to me to-night. I suppose he is afraid of her. Those straw-coloured women have dreadful tempers. Do you know, I think I'll dance with you first, Windermere. [Lord Windermere bits his lip and frowns.] It will make Lord Augustus so jealous! Lord Augustus! [Lord Augustus comes down.] Lord Windermere insists on my dancing with him first, and, as it's his own house, I can't well refuse. You know I would much sooner dance with you.

Lord Augustus. [With a low bow.] I wish I could think so, Mrs. Erlynne.

Mrs. Erlynne. You know it far too well. I can fancy a person dancing through life with you and finding it charming.

Lord Augustus. [Placing his hand on his white waistcoat.] Oh, thank you, thank you. You are the most adorable of all ladies!

Mrs. Erlynne. What a nice speech! So simple and so sincere! Just the sort of speech I like. Well, you shall hold my bouquet. [Goes towards ball-room on Lord Windermere's arm.] Ah, Mr. Dumby, how are you? I am so sorry I have been out the last three times you have called. Come and lunch on Friday.

Dumby. [With perfect nonchalance.] Delighted!

[Lady Plymdale glares with indignation at Mr. Dumby. Lord Augustus follows Mrs. Erlynne and Lord Windermere into the ball-room holding bouquet.]

Lady Plymdale. [To Mr. Dumby.] What an absolute brute you are! I never can believe a word you say! Why did you tell me you didn't know her? What do you mean by calling on her three times running? You are not to go to lunch there; of course you understand that?

Dumby. My dear Laura, I wouldn't dream of going!

Lady Plymdale. You haven't told me her name yet! Who is she?

Dumby. [Coughs slightly and smooths his hair.] She's a Mrs. Erlynne.

Lady Plymdale. That woman!

Dumby. Yes; that is what every one calls her.

Lady Plymdale. How very interesting! How intensely interesting! I really must have a good stare at her. [Goes to door of ball-room and looks in.] I have heard the most shocking things about her. They say she is ruining poor Windermere. And Lady Windermere, who goes in for being so proper, invites her! How extremely amusing! It takes a thoroughly good woman to do a thoroughly stupid thing. You are to lunch there on Friday!

Dumby. Why?

Lady Plymdale. Because I want you to take my husband with you. He has been so attentive lately, that he has become a perfect nuisance. Now, this woman is just the thing for him. He'll dance attendance upon her as long as she lets him, and won't bother me. I assure you, women of that kind are most useful. They form the basis of other people's marriages.

Dumby. What a mystery you are!

Lady Plymdale. [Looking at him.] I wish you were!

Dumby. I am—to myself. I am the only person in the world I should like to know thoroughly; but I don't see any chance of it just at present.

[They pass into the ball-room, and Lady Windermere and Lord Darlington enter from the terrace.]

Lady Windermere. Yes. Her coming here is monstrous, unbearable. I know now what you meant to-day at tea-time. Why didn't you tell me right out? You should have!

Lord Darlington. I couldn't! A man can't tell these things about another man! But if I had known he was going to make you ask her here to-night, I think I would have told you. That insult, at any rate, you would have been spared.

Lady Windermere. I did not ask her. He insisted on her coming—against my entreaties—against my commands. Oh! the house is tainted for me! I feel that every woman here sneers at me as she dances by with my husband. What have I done to deserve this? I gave him all my life. He took it—used it—spoiled it! I am degraded in my own eyes; and I lack courage—I am a coward! [Sits down on sofa.]

Lord Darlington. If I know you at all, I know that you can't live with a man who treats you like this! What sort of life would you have with him? You would feel that he was lying to you every moment of the day. You would feel that the look in his eyes was false, his voice false, his touch false, his passion false. He would come to you when he was weary of others; you would have to comfort him. He would come to you when he was devoted to others; you would have to charm him. You would have to be to him the mask of his real life, the cloak to hide his secret.

Lady Windermere. You are right—you are terribly right. But where am I to turn? You said you would be my friend, Lord Darlington.—Tell me, what am I to do? Be my friend now.

Lord Darlington. Between men and women there is no friendship possible. There is passion, enmity, worship, love, but no friendship. I love you—

Lady Windermere. No, no! [Rises.]

Lord Darlington. Yes, I love you! You are more to me than anything in the whole world. What does your husband give you? Nothing. Whatever is in him he gives to this wretched woman, whom he has thrust into your society, into your home, to shame you before every one. I offer you my life—

Lady Windermere. Lord Darlington!

Lord Darlington. My life—my whole life. Take it, and do with it what you will. . . . I love you—love you as I have never loved any living thing. From the moment I met you I loved you, loved you blindly, adoringly, madly! You did not know it then—you know it now! Leave this house to-night. I won't tell you that the world matters nothing, or the world's voice, or the voice of society. They matter a great deal. They matter far too much. But there are moments when one has to choose between living one's own life, fully, entirely, completely—or dragging out some false, shallow, degrading existence that the world in its hypocrisy demands. You have that moment now. Choose! Oh, my love, choose.

Lady Windermere. [Moving slowly away from him, and looking at him with startled eyes.] I have not the courage.

Lord Darlington. [Following her.] Yes; you have the courage. There may be six months of pain, of disgrace even, but when you no longer bear his name, when you bear mine, all will be well. Margaret, my love, my wife that shall be some day—yes, my wife! You know it! What are you now? This woman has the place that belongs by right to you. Oh! go—go out of this house, with head erect, with a smile upon your lips, with courage in your eyes. All London will know why you did it; and who will blame you? No one. If they do, what matter? Wrong? What is wrong? It's wrong for a man to abandon his wife for a shameless woman. It is wrong for a wife to remain with a man who so dishonours her. You said once you would make no compromise with things. Make none now. Be brave! Be yourself!

Lady Windermere. I am afraid of being myself. Let me think! Let me wait! My husband may return to me. [Sits down on sofa.]

Lord Darlington. And you would take him back! You are not what I thought you were. You are just the same as every other woman. You would stand anything rather than face the censure of a world, whose praise you would despise. In a week you will be driving with this woman in the Park. She will be your constant guest—your dearest friend. You would endure anything rather than break with one blow this monstrous tie. You are right. You have no courage; none!

Lady Windermere. Ah, give me time to think. I cannot answer you now. [Passes her hand nervously over her brow.]

Lord Darlington. It must be now or not at all.

Lady Windermere. [Rising from the sofa.] Then, not at all! [A pause.]

Lord Darlington. You break my heart!

Lady Windermere. Mine is already broken. [A pause.]

Lord Darlington. To-morrow I leave England. This is the last time I shall ever look on you. You will never see me again. For one moment our lives met—our souls touched. They must never meet or touch again. Good-bye, Margaret. [Exit.]

Lady Windermere. How alone I am in life! How terribly alone!

[The music stops. Enter the Duchess of Berwick and Lord Paisley laughing and talking. Other guests come on from ball-room.]

Duchess of Berwick. Dear Margaret, I've just been having such a delightful chat with Mrs. Erlynne. I am so sorry for what I said to you this afternoon about her. Of course, she must be all right if you invite her. A most attractive woman, and has such sensible views on life. Told me she entirely disapproved of people marrying more than once, so I feel quite safe about poor Augustus. Can't imagine why people speak against her. It's those horrid nieces of mine—the Saville girls—they're always talking scandal. Still, I should go to Homburg, dear, I really should. She is just a little too attractive. But where is Agatha? Oh, there she is: [Lady Agatha and Mr. Hopper enter from terrace L.U.E.] Mr. Hopper, I am very, very angry with you. You have taken Agatha out on the terrace, and she is so delicate.

Hopper. Awfully sorry, Duchess. We went out for a moment and then got chatting together.

Duchess of Berwick. [C.] Ah, about dear Australia, I suppose?

Hopper. Yes!

Duchess of Berwick. Agatha, darling! [Beckons her over.]

Lady Agatha. Yes, mamma!

Duchess of Berwick. [Aside.] Did Mr. Hopper definitely—

Lady Agatha. Yes, mamma.

Duchess of Berwick. And what answer did you give him, dear child?

Lady Agatha. Yes, mamma.

Duchess of Berwick. [Affectionately.] My dear one! You always say the right thing. Mr. Hopper! James! Agatha has told me everything. How cleverly you have both kept your secret.

Hopper. You don't mind my taking Agatha off to Australia, then, Duchess?

Duchess of Berwick. [Indignantly.] To Australia? Oh, don't mention that dreadful vulgar place.

Hopper. But she said she'd like to come with me.

Duchess of Berwick. [Severely.] Did you say that, Agatha?

Lady Agatha. Yes, mamma.

Duchess of Berwick. Agatha, you say the most silly things possible. I think on the whole that Grosvenor Square would be a more healthy place to reside in. There are lots of vulgar people live in Grosvenor Square, but at any rate there are no horrid kangaroos crawling about. But we'll talk about that to-morrow. James, you can take Agatha down. You'll come to lunch, of course, James. At half-past one, instead of two. The Duke will wish to say a few words to you, I am sure.

Hopper. I should like to have a chat with the Duke, Duchess. He has not said a single word to me yet.

Duchess of Berwick. I think you'll find he will have a great deal to say to you to-morrow. [Exit Lady Agatha with Mr. Hopper.] And now good-night, Margaret. I'm afraid it's the old, old story, dear. Love—well, not love at first sight, but love at the end of the season, which is so much more satisfactory.

Lady Windermere. Good-night, Duchess.

[Exit the Duchess of Berwick on Lord Paisley's arm.]

Lady Plymdale. My dear Margaret, what a handsome woman your husband has been dancing with! I should be quite jealous if I were you! Is she a great friend of yours?

Lady Windermere. No!

Lady Plymdale. Really? Good-night, dear. [Looks at Mr. Dumby and exit.]

Dumby. Awful manners young Hopper has!

Cecil Graham. Ah! Hopper is one of Nature's gentlemen, the worst type of gentleman I know.

Dumby. Sensible woman, Lady Windermere. Lots of wives would have objected to Mrs. Erlynne coming. But Lady Windermere has that uncommon thing called common sense.

Cecil Graham. And Windermere knows that nothing looks so like innocence as an indiscretion.

Dumby. Yes; dear Windermere is becoming almost modern. Never thought he would. [Bows to Lady Windermere and exit.]

Lady Jedburgh. Good night, Lady Windermere. What a fascinating woman Mrs. Erlynne is! She is coming to lunch on Thursday, won't you come too? I expect the Bishop and dear Lady Merton.

Lady Windermere. I am afraid I am engaged, Lady Jedburgh.

Lady Jedburgh. So sorry. Come, dear. [Exeunt Lady Jedburgh and Miss Graham.]

[Enter Mrs. Erlynne and Lord Windermere.]

Mrs. Erlynne. Charming ball it has been! Quite reminds me of old days. [Sits on sofa.] And I see that there are just as many fools in society as there used to be. So pleased to find that nothing has altered! Except Margaret. She's grown quite pretty. The last time I saw her—twenty years ago, she was a fright in flannel. Positive fright, I assure you. The dear Duchess! and that sweet Lady Agatha! Just the type of girl I like! Well, really, Windermere, if I am to be the Duchess's sister-in-law—

Lord Windermere. [Sitting L. of her.] But are you—?

[Exit Mr. Cecil Graham with rest of guests. Lady Windermere watches, with a look of scorn and pain, Mrs. Erlynne and her husband. They are unconscious of her presence.]

Mrs. Erlynne. Oh, yes! He's to call to-morrow at twelve o'clock! He wanted to propose to-night. In fact he did. He kept on proposing. Poor Augustus, you know how he repeats himself. Such a bad habit! But I told him I wouldn't give him an answer till to-morrow. Of course I am going to take him. And I dare say I'll make him an admirable wife, as wives go. And there is a great deal of good in Lord Augustus. Fortunately it is all on the surface. Just where good qualities should be. Of course you must help me in this matter.

Lord Windermere. I am not called on to encourage Lord Augustus, I suppose?

Mrs. Erlynne. Oh, no! I do the encouraging. But you will make me a handsome settlement, Windermere, won't you?

Lord Windermere. [Frowning.] Is that what you want to talk to me about to-night?

Mrs. Erlynne. Yes.

Lord Windermere. [With a gesture of impatience.] I will not talk of it here.

Mrs. Erlynne. [Laughing.] Then we will talk of it on the terrace. Even business should have a picturesque background. Should it not, Windermere? With a proper background women can do anything.

Lord Windermere. Won't to-morrow do as well?

Mrs. Erlynne. No; you see, to-morrow I am going to accept him. And I think it would be a good thing if I was able to tell him that I had—well, what shall I say?—£2000 a year left to me by a third cousin—or a second husband—or some distant relative of that kind. It would be an additional attraction, wouldn't it? You have a delightful opportunity now of paying me a compliment, Windermere. But you are not very clever at paying compliments. I am afraid Margaret doesn't encourage you in that excellent habit. It's a great mistake on her part. When men give up saying what is charming, they give up thinking what is charming. But seriously, what do you say to £2000? £2500, I think. In modern life margin is everything. Windermere, don't you think the world an intensely amusing place? I do!

[Exit on terrace with Lord Windermere. Music strikes up in ball-room.]

Lady Windermere. To stay in this house any longer is impossible. To-night a man who loves me offered me his whole life. I refused it. It was foolish of me. I will offer him mine now. I will give him mine. I will go to him! [Puts on cloak and goes to the door, then turns back. Sits down at table and writes a letter, puts it into an envelope, and leaves it on table.] Arthur has never understood me. When he reads this, he will. He may do as he chooses now with his life. I have done with mine as I think best, as I think right. It is he who has broken the bond of marriage—not I. I only break its bondage.

[Exit.]

[Parker enters L. and crosses towards the ball-room R. Enter Mrs. Erlynne.]

Mrs. Erlynne. Is Lady Windermere in the ball-room?

Parker. Her ladyship has just gone out.

Mrs. Erlynne. Gone out? She's not on the terrace?

Parker. No, madam. Her ladyship has just gone out of the house.

Mrs. Erlynne. [Starts, and looks at the servant with a puzzled expression in her face.] Out of the house?

Parker. Yes, madam—her ladyship told me she had left a letter for his lordship on the table.

Mrs. Erlynne. A letter for Lord Windermere?

Parker. Yes, madam.

Mrs. Erlynne. Thank you.

[Exit Parker. The music in the ball-room stops.] Gone out of her house! A letter addressed to her husband! [Goes over to bureau and looks at letter. Takes it up and lays it down again with a shudder of fear.] No, no! It would be impossible! Life doesn't repeat its tragedies like that! Oh, why does this horrible fancy come across me? Why do I remember now the one moment of my life I most wish to forget? Does life repeat its tragedies? [Tears letter open and reads it, then sinks down into a chair with a gesture of anguish.] Oh, how terrible! The same words that twenty years ago I wrote to her father! and how bitterly I have been punished for it! No; my punishment, my real punishment is to-night, is now! [Still seated R.]

[Enter Lord Windermere L.U.E.]

Lord Windermere. Have you said good-night to my wife? [Comes C.]

Mrs. Erlynne. [Crushing letter in her hand.] Yes.

Lord Windermere. Where is she?

Mrs. Erlynne. She is very tired. She has gone to bed. She said she had a headache.

Lord Windermere. I must go to her. You'll excuse me?

Mrs. Erlynne. [Rising hurriedly.] Oh, no! It's nothing serious. She's only very tired, that is all. Besides, there are people still in the supper-room. She wants you to make her apologies to them. She said she didn't wish to be disturbed. [Drops letter.] She asked me to tell you!

Lord Windermere. [Picks up letter.] You have dropped something.

Mrs. Erlynne. Oh yes, thank you, that is mine. [Puts out her hand to take it.]

Lord Windermere. [Still looking at letter.] But it's my wife's handwriting, isn't it?

Mrs. Erlynne. [Takes the letter quickly.] Yes, it's—an address. Will you ask them to call my carriage, please?

Lord Windermere. Certainly.

[Goes L. and Exit.]

Mrs. Erlynne. Thanks! What can I do? What can I do? I feel a passion awakening within me that I never felt before. What can it mean? The daughter must not be like the mother—that would be terrible. How can I save her? How can I save my child? A moment may ruin a life. Who knows that better than I? Windermere must be got out of the house; that is absolutely necessary. [Goes L.] But how shall I do it? It must be done somehow. Ah!

[Enter Lord Augustus R.U.E. carrying bouquet.]

Lord Augustus. Dear lady, I am in such suspense! May I not have an answer to my request?

Mrs. Erlynne. Lord Augustus, listen to me. You are to take Lord

Windermere down to your club at once, and keep him there as long as possible. You understand?

Lord Augustus. But you said you wished me to keep early hours!

Mrs. Erlynne. [Nervously.] Do what I tell you. Do what I tell you.

Lord Augustus. And my reward?

Mrs. Erlynne. Your reward? Your reward? Oh! ask me that to-morrow. But don't let Windermere out of your sight to-night. If you do I will never forgive you. I will never speak to you again. I'll have nothing to do with you. Remember you are to keep Windermere at your club, and don't let him come back to-night.

[Exit L.]

Lord Augustus. Well, really, I might be her husband already. Positively I might. [Follows her in a bewildered manner.]

ACT DROP.

THIRD ACT

SCENE

Lord Darlington's Rooms. A large sofa is in front of fireplace R. At the back of the stage a curtain is drawn across the window. Doors L. and R. Table R. with writing materials. Table C. with syphons, glasses, and Tantalus frame. Table L. with cigar and cigarette box. Lamps lit.

Lady Windermere. [Standing by the fireplace.] Why doesn't he come? This waiting is horrible. He should be here. Why is he not here, to wake by passionate words some fire within me? I am cold—cold as a loveless thing. Arthur must have read my letter by this time. If he cared for me, he would have come after me, would have taken me back by force. But he doesn't care. He's entrammelled by this woman—fascinated by her—dominated by her. If a woman wants to hold a man, she has merely to appeal to what is worst in him. We make gods of men and they leave us. Others make brutes of them and they fawn and are faithful. How hideous life is! . . . Oh! it was mad of me to come here, horribly mad. And yet, which is the worst, I wonder, to be at the mercy of a man who loves one, or the wife of a man who in one's own house dishonours one? What woman knows? What woman in the whole world? But will he love me always, this man to whom I am giving my life? What do I bring him? Lips that have lost the note of joy, eyes that are blinded by tears, chill hands and icy heart. I bring him nothing. I must go back—no; I can't go back, my letter has put me in their power—Arthur would not take me back! That fatal letter! No! Lord Darlington leaves England to-morrow. I will go with him—I have no choice. [Sits down for a few moments. Then starts up and puts on her cloak.] No, no! I will go back, let Arthur do with me what he pleases. I can't wait here. It has been madness my coming. I must go at once. As for Lord Darlington—Oh! here he is! What shall I do? What can I say to him? Will he let me go away at all? I have heard that men are brutal, horrible . . . Oh! [Hides her face in her hands.]

[Enter Mrs. Erlynne L.]

Mrs. Erlynne. Lady Windermere! [Lady Windermere starts and looks up. Then recoils in contempt.] Thank Heaven I am in time. You must go back to your husband's house immediately.

Lady Windermere. Must?

Mrs. Erlynne. [Authoritatively.] Yes, you must! There is not a second to be lost. Lord Darlington may return at any moment.

Lady Windermere. Don't come near me!

Mrs. Erlynne. Oh! You are on the brink of ruin, you are on the brink of a hideous precipice. You must leave this place at once, my carriage is waiting at the corner of the street. You must come with me and drive straight home.

[Lady Windermere throws off her cloak and flings it on the sofa.]

What are you doing?

Lady Windermere. Mrs. Erlynne—if you had not come here, I would have gone back. But now that I see you, I feel that nothing in the whole world would induce me to live under the same roof as Lord Windermere. You fill me with horror. There is something about you that stirs the wildest rage within me. And I know why you are here. My husband sent you to lure me back that I might serve as a blind to whatever relations exist between you and him.

Mrs. Erlynne. Oh! You don't think that—you can't.

Lady Windermere. Go back to my husband, Mrs. Erlynne. He belongs to you and not to me. I suppose he is afraid of a scandal. Men are such cowards. They outrage every law of the world, and are afraid of the world's tongue. But he had better prepare himself. He shall have a scandal. He shall have the worst scandal there has been in London for years. He shall see his name in every vile paper, mine on every hideous placard.

Mrs. Erlynne. No—no—

Lady Windermere. Yes! he shall. Had he come himself, I admit I would have gone back to the life of degradation you and he had prepared for me—I was going back—but to stay himself at home, and to send you as his messenger—oh! it was infamous—infamous.

Mrs. Erlynne. [C.] Lady Windermere, you wrong me horribly—you wrong your husband horribly. He doesn't know you are here—he thinks you are safe in your own house. He thinks you are asleep in your own room. He never read the mad letter you wrote to him!

Lady Windermere. [R.] Never read it!

Mrs. Erlynne. No—he knows nothing about it.

Lady Windermere. How simple you think me! [Going to her.] You are lying to me!

Mrs. Erlynne. [Restraining herself.] I am not. I am telling you the truth.

Lady Windermere. If my husband didn't read my letter, how is it that you are here? Who told you I had left the house you were shameless enough to enter? Who told you where I had gone to? My husband told you, and sent you to decoy me back. [Crosses L.]

Mrs. Erlynne. [R.C.] Your husband has never seen the letter. I—saw it, I opened it. I—read it.

Lady Windermere. [Turning to her.] You opened a letter of mine to my husband? You wouldn't dare!

Mrs. Erlynne. Dare! Oh! to save you from the abyss into which you are falling, there is nothing in the world I would not dare, nothing in the whole world. Here is the letter. Your husband has never read it. He never shall read it. [Going to fireplace.] It should never have been written. [Tears it and throws it into the fire.]

Lady Windermere. [With infinite contempt in her voice and look.] How do I know that that was my letter after all? You seem to think the commonest device can take me in!

Mrs. Erlynne. Oh! why do you disbelieve everything I tell you? What object do you think I have in coming here, except to save you from utter ruin, to save you from the consequence of a hideous mistake? That letter that is burnt now was your letter. I swear it to you!

Lady Windermere. [Slowly.] You took good care to burn it before I had examined it. I cannot trust you. You, whose whole life is a lie, could you speak the truth about anything? [Sits down.]

Mrs. Erlynne. [Hurriedly.] Think as you like about me—say what you choose against me, but go back, go back to the husband you love.

Lady Windermere. [Sullenly.] I do not love him!

Mrs. Erlynne. You do, and you know that he loves you.

Lady Windermere. He does not understand what love is. He understands it as little as you do—but I see what you want. It would be a great advantage for you to get me back. Dear Heaven! what a life I would have then! Living at the mercy of a woman who has neither mercy nor pity in her, a woman whom it is an infamy to meet, a degradation to know, a vile woman, a woman who comes between husband and wife!

Mrs. Erlynne. [With a gesture of despair.] Lady Windermere, Lady Windermere, don't say such terrible things. You don't know how terrible they are, how terrible and how unjust. Listen, you must listen! Only go back to your husband, and I promise you never to communicate with him again on any pretext—never to see him—never to have anything to do with his life or yours. The money that he gave me, he gave me not through love, but through hatred, not in worship, but in contempt. The hold I have over him—

Lady Windermere. [Rising.] Ah! you admit you have a hold!

Mrs. Erlynne. Yes, and I will tell you what it is. It is his love for you, Lady Windermere.

Lady Windermere. You expect me to believe that?

Mrs. Erlynne. You must believe it! It is true. It is his love for you that has made him submit to—oh! call it what you like, tyranny, threats, anything you choose. But it is his love for you. His desire to spare you—shame, yes, shame and disgrace.

Lady Windermere. What do you mean? You are insolent! What have I to do with you?

Mrs. Erlynne. [Humbly.] Nothing. I know it—but I tell you that your husband loves you—that you may never meet with such love again in your whole life—that such love you will never meet—and that if you throw it away, the day may come when you will starve for love and it will not be given to you, beg for love and it will be denied you—Oh! Arthur loves you!

Lady Windermere. Arthur? And you tell me there is nothing between you?

Mrs. Erlynne. Lady Windermere, before Heaven your husband is guiltless of all offence towards you! And I—I tell you that had it ever occurred to me that such a monstrous suspicion would have entered your mind, I would have died rather than have crossed your life or his—oh! died, gladly died! [Moves away to sofa R.]

Lady Windermere. You talk as if you had a heart. Women like you have no hearts. Heart is not in you. You are bought and sold. [Sits L.C.]

Mrs. Erlynne. [Starts, with a gesture of pain. Then restrains herself, and comes over to where Lady Windermere is sitting. As she speaks, she stretches out her hands towards her, but does not dare to touch her.] Believe what you choose about me. I am not worth a moment's sorrow. But don't spoil your beautiful young life on my account! You don't know what may be in store for you, unless you leave this house at once. You don't know what it is to fall into the pit, to be despised, mocked, abandoned, sneered at—to be an outcast! to find the door shut against one, to have to creep in by hideous byways, afraid every moment lest the mask should be stripped from one's face, and all the while to hear the laughter, the horrible laughter of the world, a thing more tragic than all the tears the world has ever shed. You don't know what it is. One pays for one's sin, and then one pays again, and all one's life one pays. You must never know that.—As for me, if suffering be an expiation, then at this moment I have expiated all my faults, whatever they have been; for to-night you have made a heart in one who had it not, made it and broken it.—But let that pass. I may have wrecked my own life, but I will not let you wreck yours. You—why, you are a mere girl, you would be lost. You haven't got the kind of brains that enables a woman to get back. You have neither the wit nor the courage. You couldn't stand dishonour! No! Go back, Lady Windermere, to the husband who loves you, whom you love. You have a child, Lady Windermere. Go back to that child who even now, in pain or in joy, may be calling to you. [Lady Windermere rises.] God gave you that child. He will require from you that you make his life fine, that you watch over him. What answer will you make to God if his life is ruined through you? Back to your house, Lady Windermere—your husband loves you! He has never swerved for a moment from the love he bears you. But even if he had a thousand loves, you must stay with your child. If he was harsh to you, you must stay with your child. If he ill-treated you, you must stay with your child. If he abandoned you, your place is with your child.

[Lady Windermere bursts into tears and buries her face in her hands.]

[Rushing to her.] Lady Windermere!

Lady Windermere. [Holding out her hands to her, helplessly, as a child might do.] Take me home. Take me home.

Mrs. Erlynne. [Is about to embrace her. Then restrains herself. There is a look of wonderful joy in her face.] Come! Where is your cloak? [Getting it from sofa.] Here. Put it on. Come at once!

[They go to the door.]

Lady Windermere. Stop! Don't you hear voices?

Mrs. Erlynne. No, no! There was no one!

Lady Windermere. Yes, there is! Listen! Oh! that is my husband's voice! He is coming in! Save me! Oh, it's some plot! You have sent for him.

[Voices outside.]

Mrs. Erlynne. Silence! I'm here to save you, if I can. But I fear it is too late! There! [Points to the curtain across the window.] The first chance you have, slip out, if you ever get a chance!

Lady Windermere. But you?

Mrs. Erlynne. Oh! never mind me. I'll face them.

[Lady Windermere hides herself behind the curtain.]

Lord Augustus. [Outside.] Nonsense, dear Windermere, you must not leave me!

Mrs. Erlynne. Lord Augustus! Then it is I who am lost! [Hesitates for a moment, then looks round and sees door R., and exits through it.]

[Enter Lord Darlington, Mr. Dumby, Lord Windermere, Lord Augustus Lorton, and Mr. Cecil Graham.

Dumby. What a nuisance their turning us out of the club at this hour! It's only two o'clock. [Sinks into a chair.] The lively part of the evening is only just beginning. [Yawns and closes his eyes.]

Lord Windermere. It is very good of you, Lord Darlington, allowing Augustus to force our company on you, but I'm afraid I can't stay long.

Lord Darlington. Really! I am so sorry! You'll take a cigar, won't you?

Lord Windermere. Thanks! [Sits down.]

Lord Augustus. [To Lord Windermere.] My dear boy, you must not dream of going. I have a great deal to talk to you about, of demmed importance, too. [Sits down with him at L. table.]

Cecil Graham. Oh! We all know what that is! Tuppy can't talk about anything but Mrs. Erlynne.

Lord Windermere. Well, that is no business of yours, is it, Cecil?

Cecil Graham. None! That is why it interests me. My own business always bores me to death. I prefer other people's.

Lord Darlington. Have something to drink, you fellows. Cecil, you'll have a whisky and soda?

Cecil Graham. Thanks. [Goes to table with Lord Darlington.] Mrs. Erlynne looked very handsome to-night, didn't she?

Lord Darlington. I am not one of her admirers.

Cecil Graham. I usen't to be, but I am now. Why! she actually made me introduce her to poor dear Aunt Caroline. I believe she is going to lunch there.

Lord Darlington. [In Purple.] No?

Cecil Graham. She is, really.

Lord Darlington. Excuse me, you fellows. I'm going away to-morrow. And I have to write a few letters. [Goes to writing table and sits down.]

Dumby. Clever woman, Mrs. Erlynne.

Cecil Graham. Hallo, Dumby! I thought you were asleep.

Dumby. I am, I usually am!

Lord Augustus. A very clever woman. Knows perfectly well what a demmed fool I am—knows it as well as I do myself.

[Cecil Graham comes towards him laughing.]

Ah, you may laugh, my boy, but it is a great thing to come across a woman who thoroughly understands one.

Dumby. It is an awfully dangerous thing. They always end by marrying one.

Cecil Graham. But I thought, Tuppy, you were never going to see her again! Yes! you told me so yesterday evening at the club. You said you'd heard—

[Whispering to him.]

Lord Augustus. Oh, she's explained that.

Cecil Graham. And the Wiesbaden affair?

Lord Augustus. She's explained that too.

Dumby. And her income, Tuppy? Has she explained that?

Lord Augustus. [In a very serious voice.] She's going to explain that to-morrow.

[Cecil Graham goes back to C. table.]

Dumby. Awfully commercial, women nowadays. Our grandmothers threw their caps over the mills, of course, but, by Jove, their granddaughters only throw their caps over mills that can raise the wind for them.

Lord Augustus. You want to make her out a wicked woman. She is not!

Cecil Graham. Oh! Wicked women bother one. Good women bore one. That is the only difference between them.

Lord Augustus. [Puffing a cigar.] Mrs. Erlynne has a future before her.

Dumby. Mrs. Erlynne has a past before her.

Lord Augustus. I prefer women with a past. They're always so demmed amusing to talk to.

Cecil Graham. Well, you'll have lots of topics of conversation with her, Tuppy. [Rising and going to him.]

Lord Augustus. You're getting annoying, dear-boy; you're getting demmed annoying.

Cecil Graham. [Puts his hands on his shoulders.] Now, Tuppy, you've lost your figure and you've lost your character. Don't lose your temper; you have only got one.

Lord Augustus. My dear boy, if I wasn't the most good-natured man in London—

Cecil Graham. We'd treat you with more respect, wouldn't we, Tuppy? [Strolls away.]

Dumby. The youth of the present day are quite monstrous. They have absolutely no respect for dyed hair. [Lord Augustus looks round angrily.]

Cecil Graham. Mrs. Erlynne has a very great respect for dear Tuppy.

Dumby. Then Mrs. Erlynne sets an admirable example to the rest of her sex. It is perfectly brutal the way most women nowadays behave to men who are not their husbands.

Lord Windermere. Dumby, you are ridiculous, and Cecil, you let your tongue run away with you. You must leave Mrs. Erlynne alone. You don't really know anything about her, and you're always talking scandal against her.

Cecil Graham. [Coming towards him L.C.] My dear Arthur, I never talk scandal. I only talk gossip.

Lord Windermere. What is the difference between scandal and gossip?

Cecil Graham. Oh! gossip is charming! History is merely gossip. But scandal is gossip made tedious by morality. Now, I never moralise. A man who moralises is usually a hypocrite, and a woman who moralises is invariably plain. There is nothing in the whole world so unbecoming to a woman as a Nonconformist conscience. And most women know it, I'm glad to say.

Lord Augustus. Just my sentiments, dear boy, just my sentiments.

Cecil Graham. Sorry to hear it, Tuppy; whenever people agree with me, I always feel I must be wrong.

Lord Augustus. My dear boy, when I was your age—

Cecil Graham. But you never were, Tuppy, and you never will be. [Goes up C.] I say, Darlington, let us have some cards. You'll play, Arthur, won't you?

Lord Windermere. No, thanks, Cecil.

Dumby. [With a sigh.] Good heavens! how marriage ruins a man! It's as demoralising as cigarettes, and far more expensive.

Cecil Graham. You'll play, of course, Tuppy?

Lord Augustus. [Pouring himself out a brandy and soda at table.] Can't, dear boy. Promised Mrs. Erlynne never to play or drink again.

Cecil Graham. Now, my dear Tuppy, don't be led astray into the paths of virtue. Reformed, you would be perfectly tedious. That is the worst of women. They always want one to be good. And if we are good, when they meet us, they don't love us at all. They like to find us quite irretrievably bad, and to leave us quite unattractively good.

Lord Darlington. [Rising from R. table, where he has been writing letters.] They always do find us bad!

Dumby. I don't think we are bad. I think we are all good, except Tuppy.

Lord Darlington. No, we are all in the gutter, but some of us are looking at the stars. [Sits down at C. table.]

Dumby. We are all in the gutter, but some of us are looking at the stars? Upon my word, you are very romantic to-night, Darlington.

Cecil Graham. Too romantic! You must be in love. Who is the girl?

Lord Darlington. The woman I love is not free, or thinks she isn't. [Glances instinctively at Lord Windermere while he speaks.]

Cecil Graham. A married woman, then! Well, there's nothing in the world like the devotion of a married woman. It's a thing no married man knows anything about.

Lord Darlington. Oh! she doesn't love me. She is a good woman. She is the only good woman I have ever met in my life.

Cecil Graham. The only good woman you have ever met in your life?

Lord Darlington. Yes!

Cecil Graham. [Lighting a cigarette.] Well, you are a lucky fellow! Why, I have met hundreds of good women. I never seem to meet any but good women. The world is perfectly packed with good women. To know them is a middle-class education.

Lord Darlington. This woman has purity and innocence. She has everything we men have lost.

Cecil Graham. My dear fellow, what on earth should we men do going about with purity and innocence? A carefully thought-out buttonhole is much more effective.

Dumby. She doesn't really love you then?

Lord Darlington. No, she does not!

Dumby. I congratulate you, my dear fellow. In this world there are only two tragedies. One is not getting what one wants, and the other is getting it. The last is much the worst; the last is a real tragedy! But I am interested to hear she does not love you. How long could you love a woman who didn't love you, Cecil?

Cecil Graham. A woman who didn't love me? Oh, all my life!

Dumby. So could I. But it's so difficult to meet one.

Lord Darlington. How can you be so conceited, Dumby?

Dumby. I didn't say it as a matter of conceit. I said it as a matter of regret. I have been wildly, madly adored. I am sorry I have. It has been an immense nuisance. I should like to be allowed a little time to myself now and then.

Lord Augustus. [Looking round.] Time to educate yourself, I suppose.

Dumby. No, time to forget all I have learned. That is much more important, dear Tuppy. [Lord Augustus moves uneasily in his chair.]

Lord Darlington. What cynics you fellows are!

Cecil Graham. What is a cynic? [Sitting on the back of the sofa.]

Lord Darlington. A man who knows the price of everything and the value of nothing.

Cecil Graham. And a sentimentalist, my dear Darlington, is a man who sees an absurd value in everything, and doesn't know the market price of any single thing.

Lord Darlington. You always amuse me, Cecil. You talk as if you were a man of experience.

Cecil Graham. I am. [Moves up to front off fireplace.]

Lord Darlington. You are far too young!

Cecil Graham. That is a great error. Experience is a question of instinct about life. I have got it. Tuppy hasn't. Experience is the name Tuppy gives to his mistakes. That is all. [Lord Augustus looks round indignantly.]

Dumby. Experience is the name every one gives to their mistakes.

Cecil Graham. [Standing with his back to the fireplace.] One shouldn't commit any. [Sees Lady Windermere's fan on sofa.]

Dumby. Life would be very dull without them.

Cecil Graham. Of course you are quite faithful to this woman you are in love with, Darlington, to this good woman?

Lord Darlington. Cecil, if one really loves a woman, all other women in the world become absolutely meaningless to one. Love changes one—I am changed.

Cecil Graham. Dear me! How very interesting! Tuppy, I want to talk to you. [Lord Augustus takes no notice.]

Dumby. It's no use talking to Tuppy. You might just as well talk to a brick wall.

Cecil Graham. But I like talking to a brick wall—it's the only thing in the world that never contradicts me! Tuppy!

Lord Augustus. Well, what is it? What is it? [Rising and going over to Cecil Graham.]

Cecil Graham. Come over here. I want you particularly. [Aside.]

Darlington has been moralising and talking about the purity of love, and that sort of thing, and he has got some woman in his rooms all the time.

Lord Augustus. No, really! really!

Cecil Graham. [In a low voice.] Yes, here is her fan. [Points to the fan.]

Lord Augustus. [Chuckling.] By Jove! By Jove!

Lord Windermere. [Up by door.] I am really off now, Lord Darlington. I am sorry you are leaving England so soon. Pray call on us when you come back! My wife and I will be charmed to see you!

Lord Darlington. [Upstage with Lord Windermere.] I am afraid I shall be away for many years. Good-night!

Cecil Graham. Arthur!

Lord Windermere. What?

Cecil Graham. I want to speak to you for a moment. No, do come!

Lord Windermere. [Putting on his coat.] I can't—I'm off!

Cecil Graham. It is something very particular. It will interest you enormously.

Lord Windermere. [Smiling.] It is some of your nonsense, Cecil.

Cecil Graham. It isn't! It isn't really.

Lord Augustus. [Going to him.] My dear fellow, you mustn't go yet. I have a lot to talk to you about. And Cecil has something to show you.

Lord Windermere. [Walking over.] Well, what is it?

Cecil Graham. Darlington has got a woman here in his rooms. Here is her fan. Amusing, isn't it? [A pause.]

Lord Windermere. Good God! [Seizes the fan—Dumby rises.]

Cecil Graham. What is the matter?

Lord Windermere. Lord Darlington!

Lord Darlington. [Turning round.] Yes!

Lord Windermere. What is my wife's fan doing here in your rooms? Hands off, Cecil. Don't touch me.

Lord Darlington. Your wife's fan?

Lord Windermere. Yes, here it is!

Lord Darlington. [Walking towards him.] I don't know!

Lord Windermere. You must know. I demand an explanation. Don't hold me, you fool. [To Cecil Graham.]

Lord Darlington. [Aside.] She is here after all!

Lord Windermere. Speak, sir! Why is my wife's fan here? Answer me! By God! I'll search your rooms, and if my wife's here, I'll— [Moves.]

Lord Darlington. You shall not search my rooms. You have no right to do so. I forbid you!

Lord Windermere. You scoundrel! I'll not leave your room till I have searched every corner of it! What moves behind that curtain? [Rushes towards the curtain C.]

Mrs. Erlynne. [Enters behind R.] Lord Windermere!

Lord Windermere. Mrs. Erlynne!

[Every one starts and turns round. Lady Windermere slips out from behind the curtain and glides from the room L.]

Mrs. Erlynne. I am afraid I took your wife's fan in mistake for my own, when I was leaving your house to-night. I am so sorry. [Takes fan from him. Lord Windermere looks at her in contempt. Lord Darlington in mingled astonishment and anger. Lord Augustus turns away. The other men smile at each other.]

Act Drop.

FOURTH ACT

SCENE—Same as in Act I.

Lady Windermere. [Lying on sofa.] How can I tell him? I can't tell him. It would kill me. I wonder what happened after I escaped from that horrible room. Perhaps she told them the true reason of her being there, and the real meaning of that—fatal fan of mine. Oh, if he knows—how can I look him in the face again? He would never forgive me. [Touches bell.] How securely one thinks one lives—out of reach of temptation, sin, folly. And then suddenly—Oh! Life is terrible. It rules us, we do not rule it.

[Enter Rosalie R.]

Rosalie. Did your ladyship ring for me?

Lady Windermere. Yes. Have you found out at what time Lord Windermere came in last night?

Rosalie. His lordship did not come in till five o'clock.

Lady Windermere. Five o'clock? He knocked at my door this morning, didn't he?

Rosalie. Yes, my lady—at half-past nine. I told him your ladyship was not awake yet.

Lady Windermere. Did he say anything?

Rosalie. Something about your ladyship's fan. I didn't quite catch what his lordship said. Has the fan been lost, my lady? I can't find it, and Parker says it was not left in any of the rooms. He has looked in all of them and on the terrace as well.

Lady Windermere. It doesn't matter. Tell Parker not to trouble. That will do.

[Exit Rosalie.]

Lady Windermere. [Rising.] She is sure to tell him. I can fancy a person doing a wonderful act of self-sacrifice, doing it spontaneously, recklessly, nobly—and afterwards finding out that it costs too much. Why should she hesitate between her ruin and mine? . . . How strange! I would have publicly disgraced her in my own house. She accepts public disgrace in the house of another to save me. . . . There is a bitter irony in things, a bitter irony in the way we talk of good and bad women. . . . Oh, what a lesson! and what a pity that in life we only get our lessons when they are of no use to us! For even if she doesn't tell, I must. Oh! the shame of it, the shame of it. To tell it is to live through it all again. Actions are the first tragedy in life, words are the second. Words are perhaps the worst. Words are merciless. . . . Oh! [Starts as Lord Windermere enters.]

Lord Windermere. [Kisses her.] Margaret—how pale you look!

Lady Windermere. I slept very badly.

Lord Windermere. [Sitting on sofa with her.] I am so sorry. I came in dreadfully late, and didn't like to wake you. You are crying, dear.

Lady Windermere. Yes, I am crying, for I have something to tell you, Arthur.

Lord Windermere. My dear child, you are not well. You've been doing too much. Let us go away to the country. You'll be all right at Selby. The season is almost over. There is no use staying on. Poor darling! We'll go away to-day, if you like. [Rises.] We can easily catch the 3.40. I'll send a wire to Fannen. [Crosses and sits down at table to write a telegram.]

Lady Windermere. Yes; let us go away to-day. No; I can't go to-day, Arthur. There is some one I must see before I leave town—some one who has been kind to me.

Lord Windermere. [Rising and leaning over sofa.] Kind to you?

Lady Windermere. Far more than that. [Rises and goes to him.] I will tell you, Arthur, but only love me, love me as you used to love me.

Lord Windermere. Used to? You are not thinking of that wretched woman who came here last night? [Coming round and sitting R. of her.] You don't still imagine—no, you couldn't.

Lady Windermere. I don't. I know now I was wrong and foolish.

Lord Windermere. It was very good of you to receive her last night—but you are never to see her again.

Lady Windermere. Why do you say that? [A pause.]

Lord Windermere. [Holding her hand.] Margaret, I thought Mrs. Erlynne was a woman more sinned against than sinning, as the phrase goes. I thought she wanted to be good, to get back into a place that she had lost by a moment's folly, to lead again a decent life. I believed what she told me—I was mistaken in her. She is bad—as bad as a woman can be.

Lady Windermere. Arthur, Arthur, don't talk so bitterly about any woman. I don't think now that people can be divided into the good and the bad as though they were two separate races or creations. What are called good women may have terrible things in them, mad moods of recklessness, assertion, jealousy, sin. Bad women, as they are termed, may have in them sorrow, repentance, pity, sacrifice. And I don't think Mrs. Erlynne a bad woman—I know she's not.

Lord Windermere. My dear child, the woman's impossible. No matter what harm she tries to do us, you must never see her again. She is inadmissible anywhere.

Lady Windermere. But I want to see her. I want her to come here.

Lord Windermere. Never!

Lady Windermere. She came here once as your guest. She must come now as mine. That is but fair.

Lord Windermere. She should never have come here.

Lady Windermere. [Rising.] It is too late, Arthur, to say that now. [Moves away.]

Lord Windermere. [Rising.] Margaret, if you knew where Mrs. Erlynne went last night, after she left this house, you would not sit in the same room with her. It was absolutely shameless, the whole thing.

Lady Windermere. Arthur, I can't bear it any longer. I must tell you. Last night—

[Enter Parker with a tray on which lie Lady Windermere's fan and a card.]

Parker. Mrs. Erlynne has called to return your ladyship's fan which she took away by mistake last night. Mrs. Erlynne has written a message on the card.

Lady Windermere. Oh, ask Mrs. Erlynne to be kind enough to come up. [Reads card.] Say I shall be very glad to see her.

[Exit Parker.]

She wants to see me, Arthur.

Lord Windermere. [Takes card and looks at it.] Margaret, I beg you not to. Let me see her first, at any rate. She's a very dangerous woman. She is the most dangerous woman I know. You don't realise what you're doing.

Lady Windermere. It is right that I should see her.

Lord Windermere. My child, you may be on the brink of a great sorrow. Don't go to meet it. It is absolutely necessary that I should see her before you do.

Lady Windermere. Why should it be necessary?

[Enter Parker.]

Parker. Mrs. Erlynne.

[Enter Mrs. Erlynne.]

[Exit Parker.]

Mrs. Erlynne. How do you do, Lady Windermere? [To Lord Windermere.] How do you do? Do you know, Lady Windermere, I am so sorry about your fan. I can't imagine how I made such a silly mistake. Most stupid of me. And as I was driving in your direction, I thought I would take the opportunity of returning your property in person with many apologies for my carelessness, and of bidding you good-bye.

Lady Windermere. Good-bye? [Moves towards sofa with Mrs. Erlynne and sits down beside her.] Are you going away, then, Mrs. Erlynne?

Mrs. Erlynne. Yes; I am going to live abroad again. The English climate doesn't suit me. My—heart is affected here, and that I don't like. I prefer living in the south. London is too full of fogs and—and serious people, Lord Windermere. Whether the fogs produce the serious people or whether the serious people produce the fogs, I don't know, but the whole thing rather gets on my nerves, and so I'm leaving this afternoon by the Club Train.

Lady Windermere. This afternoon? But I wanted so much to come and see you.

Mrs. Erlynne. How kind of you! But I am afraid I have to go.

Lady Windermere. Shall I never see you again, Mrs. Erlynne?

Mrs. Erlynne. I am afraid not. Our lives lie too far apart. But there is a little thing I would like you to do for me. I want a photograph of you, Lady Windermere—would you give me one? You don't know how gratified I should be.

Lady Windermere. Oh, with pleasure. There is one on that table. I'll show it to you. [Goes across to the table.]

Lord Windermere. [Coming up to Mrs. Erlynne and speaking in a low voice.] It is monstrous your intruding yourself here after your conduct last night.

Mrs. Erlynne. [With an amused smile.] My dear Windermere, manners before morals!

Lady Windermere. [Returning.] I'm afraid it is very flattering—I am not so pretty as that. [Showing photograph.]

Mrs. Erlynne. You are much prettier. But haven't you got one of yourself with your little boy?

Lady Windermere. I have. Would you prefer one of those?

Mrs. Erlynne. Yes.

Lady Windermere. I'll go and get it for you, if you'll excuse me for a moment. I have one upstairs.

Mrs. Erlynne. So sorry, Lady Windermere, to give you so much trouble.

Lady Windermere. [Moves to door R.] No trouble at all, Mrs. Erlynne.

Mrs. Erlynne. Thanks so much.

[Exit Lady Windermere R.] You seem rather out of temper this morning, Windermere. Why should you be? Margaret and I get on charmingly together.

Lord Windermere. I can't bear to see you with her. Besides, you have not told me the truth, Mrs. Erlynne.

Mrs. Erlynne. I have not told her the truth, you mean.

Lord Windermere. [Standing C.] I sometimes wish you had. I should have been spared then the misery, the anxiety, the annoyance of the last six months. But rather than my wife should know—that the mother whom she was taught to consider as dead, the mother whom she has mourned as dead, is living—a divorced woman, going about under an assumed name, a bad woman preying upon life, as I know you now to be—rather than that, I was ready to supply you with money to pay bill after bill, extravagance after extravagance, to risk what occurred yesterday, the first quarrel I have ever had with my wife. You don't understand what that means to me. How could you? But I tell you that the only bitter words that ever came from those sweet lips of hers were on your account, and I hate to see you next her. You sully the innocence that is in her. [Moves L.C.] And then I used to think that with all your faults you were frank and honest. You are not.

Mrs. Erlynne. Why do you say that?

Lord Windermere. You made me get you an invitation to my wife's ball.

Mrs. Erlynne. For my daughter's ball—yes.

Lord Windermere. You came, and within an hour of your leaving the house you are found in a man's rooms—you are disgraced before every one. [Goes up stage C.]

Mrs. Erlynne. Yes.

Lord Windermere. [Turning round on her.] Therefore I have a right to look upon you as what you are—a worthless, vicious woman. I have the right to tell you never to enter this house, never to attempt to come near my wife—

Mrs. Erlynne. [Coldly.] My daughter, you mean.

Lord Windermere. You have no right to claim her as your daughter. You left her, abandoned her when she was but a child in the cradle, abandoned her for your lover, who abandoned you in turn.

Mrs. Erlynne. [Rising.] Do you count that to his credit, Lord Windermere—or to mine?

Lord Windermere. To his, now that I know you.

Mrs. Erlynne. Take care—you had better be careful.

Lord Windermere. Oh, I am not going to mince words for you. I know you thoroughly.

Mrs. Erlynne. [Looks steadily at him.] I question that.

Lord Windermere. I do know you. For twenty years of your life you lived without your child, without a thought of your child. One day you read in the papers that she had married a rich man. You saw your hideous chance. You knew that to spare her the ignominy of learning that a woman like you was her mother, I would endure anything. You began your blackmailing.

Mrs. Erlynne. [Shrugging her shoulders.] Don't use ugly words, Windermere. They are vulgar. I saw my chance, it is true, and took it.

Lord Windermere. Yes, you took it—and spoiled it all last night by being found out.

Mrs. Erlynne. [With a strange smile.] You are quite right, I spoiled it all last night.

Lord Windermere. And as for your blunder in taking my wife's fan from here and then leaving it about in Darlington's rooms, it is unpardonable. I can't bear the sight of it now. I shall never let my wife use it again. The thing is soiled for me. You should have kept it and not brought it back.

Mrs. Erlynne. I think I shall keep it. [Goes up.] It's extremely pretty. [Takes up fan.] I shall ask Margaret to give it to me.

Lord Windermere. I hope my wife will give it you.

Mrs. Erlynne. Oh, I'm sure she will have no objection.

Lord Windermere. I wish that at the same time she would give you a miniature she kisses every night before she prays—It's the miniature of a young innocent-looking girl with beautiful dark hair.

Mrs. Erlynne. Ah, yes, I remember. How long ago that seems! [Goes to sofa and sits down.] It was done before I was married. Dark hair and an innocent expression were the fashion then, Windermere! [A pause.]

Lord Windermere. What do you mean by coming here this morning? What is your object? [Crossing L.C. and sitting.]

Mrs. Erlynne. [With a note of irony in her voice.] To bid good-bye to my dear daughter, of course. [Lord Windermere bites his under lip in anger. Mrs. Erlynne looks at him, and her voice and manner become serious. In her accents at she talks there is a note of deep tragedy. For a moment she reveals herself.] Oh, don't imagine I am going to have a pathetic scene with her, weep on her neck and tell her who I am, and all that kind of thing. I have no ambition to play the part of a mother. Only once in my life have I known a mother's feelings. That was last night. They were terrible—they made me suffer—they made me suffer too much. For twenty years, as you say, I have lived childless,—I want to live childless still. [Hiding her feelings with a trivial laugh.] Besides, my dear Windermere, how on earth could I pose as a mother with a grown-up daughter? Margaret is twenty-one, and I have never admitted that I am more than twenty-nine, or thirty at the most. Twenty-nine when there are pink shades, thirty when there are not. So you see what difficulties it would involve. No, as far as I am concerned, let your wife cherish the memory of this dead, stainless mother. Why should I interfere with her illusions? I find it hard enough to keep my own. I lost one illusion last night. I thought I had no heart. I find I have, and a heart doesn't suit me, Windermere. Somehow it doesn't go with modern dress. It makes one look old. [Takes up hand-mirror from table and looks into it.] And it spoils one's career at critical moments.

Lord Windermere. You fill me with horror—with absolute horror.

Mrs. Erlynne. [Rising.] I suppose, Windermere, you would like me to retire into a convent, or become a hospital nurse, or something of that kind, as people do in silly modern novels. That is stupid of you, Arthur; in real life we don't do such things—not as long as we have any good looks left, at any rate. No—what consoles one nowadays is not repentance, but pleasure. Repentance is quite out of date. And besides, if a woman really repents, she has to go to a bad dressmaker, otherwise no one believes in her. And nothing in the world would induce me to do that. No; I am going to pass entirely out of your two lives. My coming into them has been a mistake—I discovered that last night.

Lord Windermere. A fatal mistake.

Mrs. Erlynne. [Smiling.] Almost fatal.

Lord Windermere. I am sorry now I did not tell my wife the whole thing at once.

Mrs. Erlynne. I regret my bad actions. You regret your good ones—that is the difference between us.

Lord Windermere. I don't trust you. I will tell my wife. It's better for her to know, and from me. It will cause her infinite pain—it will humiliate her terribly, but it's right that she should know.

Mrs. Erlynne. You propose to tell her?

Lord Windermere. I am going to tell her.

Mrs. Erlynne. [Going up to him.] If you do, I will make my name so infamous that it will mar every moment of her life. It will ruin her, and make her wretched. If you dare to tell her, there is no depth of degradation I will not sink to, no pit of shame I will not enter. You shall not tell her—I forbid you.

Lord Windermere. Why?

Mrs. Erlynne. [After a pause.] If I said to you that I cared for her, perhaps loved her even—you would sneer at me, wouldn't you?

Lord Windermere. I should feel it was not true. A mother's love means devotion, unselfishness, sacrifice. What could you know of such things?

Mrs. Erlynne. You are right. What could I know of such things? Don't let us talk any more about it—as for telling my daughter who I am, that I do not allow. It is my secret, it is not yours. If I make up my mind to tell her, and I think I will, I shall tell her before I leave the house—if not, I shall never tell her.

Lord Windermere. [Angrily.] Then let me beg of you to leave our house at once. I will make your excuses to Margaret.

[Enter Lady Windermere R. She goes over to Mrs. Erlynne with the photograph in her hand. Lord Windermere moves to back of sofa, and anxiously watches Mrs. Erlynne as the scene progresses.]

Lady Windermere. I am so sorry, Mrs. Erlynne, to have kept you waiting. I couldn't find the photograph anywhere. At last I discovered it in my husband's dressing-room—he had stolen it.

Mrs. Erlynne. [Takes the photograph from her and looks at it.] I am not surprised—it is charming. [Goes over to sofa with Lady Windermere, and sits down beside her. Looks again at the photograph.] And so that is your little boy! What is he called?

Lady Windermere. Gerard, after my dear father.

Mrs. Erlynne. [Laying the photograph down.] Really?

Lady Windermere. Yes. If it had been a girl, I would have called it after my mother. My mother had the same name as myself, Margaret.

Mrs. Erlynne. My name is Margaret too.

Lady Windermere. Indeed!

Mrs. Erlynne. Yes. [Pause.] You are devoted to your mother's memory, Lady Windermere, your husband tells me.

Lady Windermere. We all have ideals in life. At least we all should have. Mine is my mother.

Mrs. Erlynne. Ideals are dangerous things. Realities are better. They wound, but they're better.

Lady Windermere. [Shaking her head.] If I lost my ideals, I should lose everything.

Mrs. Erlynne. Everything?

Lady Windermere. Yes. [Pause.]

Mrs. Erlynne. Did your father often speak to you of your mother?

Lady Windermere. No, it gave him too much pain. He told me how my mother had died a few months after I was born. His eyes filled with tears as he spoke. Then he begged me never to mention her name to him again. It made him suffer even to hear it. My father—my father really died of a broken heart. His was the most ruined life know.

Mrs. Erlynne. [Rising.] I am afraid I must go now, Lady Windermere.

Lady Windermere. [Rising.] Oh no, don't.

Mrs. Erlynne. I think I had better. My carriage must have come back by this time. I sent it to Lady Jedburgh's with a note.

Lady Windermere. Arthur, would you mind seeing if Mrs. Erlynne's carriage has come back?

Mrs. Erlynne. Pray don't trouble, Lord Windermere.

Lady Windermere. Yes, Arthur, do go, please.

[Lord Windermere hesitated for a moment and looks at Mrs. Erlynne. She remains quite impassive. He leaves the room.]

[To Mrs. Erlynne.] Oh! What am I to say to you? You saved me last night? [Goes towards her.]

Mrs. Erlynne. Hush—don't speak of it.

Lady Windermere. I must speak of it. I can't let you think that I am going to accept this sacrifice. I am not. It is too great. I am going to tell my husband everything. It is my duty.

Mrs. Erlynne. It is not your duty—at least you have duties to others besides him. You say you owe me something?

Lady Windermere. I owe you everything.

Mrs. Erlynne. Then pay your debt by silence. That is the only way in which it can be paid. Don't spoil the one good thing I have done in my life by telling it to any one. Promise me that what passed last night will remain a secret between us. You must not bring misery into your husband's life. Why spoil his love? You must not spoil it. Love is easily killed. Oh! how easily love is killed. Pledge me your word, Lady Windermere, that you will never tell him. I insist upon it.

Lady Windermere. [With bowed head.] It is your will, not mine.

Mrs. Erlynne. Yes, it is my will. And never forget your child—I like to think of you as a mother. I like you to think of yourself as one.

Lady Windermere. [Looking up.] I always will now. Only once in my life I have forgotten my own mother—that was last night. Oh, if I had remembered her I should not have been so foolish, so wicked.

Mrs. Erlynne. [With a slight shudder.] Hush, last night is quite over.

[Enter Lord Windermere.]

Lord Windermere. Your carriage has not come back yet, Mrs. Erlynne.

Mrs. Erlynne. It makes no matter. I'll take a hansom. There is nothing in the world so respectable as a good Shrewsbury and Talbot. And now, dear Lady Windermere, I am afraid it is really good-bye. [Moves up C.] Oh, I remember. You'll think me absurd, but do you know I've taken a great fancy to this fan that I was silly enough to run away with last night from your ball. Now, I wonder would you give it to me? Lord Windermere says you may. I know it is his present.

Lady Windermere. Oh, certainly, if it will give you any pleasure. But it has my name on it. It has 'Margaret' on it.

Mrs. Erlynne. But we have the same Christian name.

Lady Windermere. Oh, I forgot. Of course, do have it. What a wonderful chance our names being the same!

Mrs. Erlynne. Quite wonderful. Thanks—it will always remind me of you. [Shakes hands with her.]

[Enter Parker.]

Parker. Lord Augustus Lorton. Mrs. Erlynne's carriage has come.

[Enter Lord Augustus.]

Lord Augustus. Good morning, dear boy. Good morning, Lady Windermere. [Sees Mrs. Erlynne.] Mrs. Erlynne!

Mrs. Erlynne. How do you do, Lord Augustus? Are you quite well this morning?

Lord Augustus. [Coldly.] Quite well, thank you, Mrs. Erlynne.

Mrs. Erlynne. You don't look at all well, Lord Augustus. You stop up too late—it is so bad for you. You really should take more care of yourself. Good-bye, Lord Windermere. [Goes towards door with a bow to Lord Augustus. Suddenly smiles and looks back at him.] Lord Augustus! Won't you see me to my carriage? You might carry the fan.

Lord Windermere. Allow me!

Mrs. Erlynne. No; I want Lord Augustus. I have a special message for the dear Duchess. Won't you carry the fan, Lord Augustus?

Lord Augustus. If you really desire it, Mrs. Erlynne.

Mrs. Erlynne. [Laughing.] Of course I do. You'll carry it so gracefully. You would carry off anything gracefully, dear Lord Augustus.

[When she reaches the door she looks back for a moment at Lady Windermere. Their eyes meet. Then she turns, and exit C. followed by Lord Augustus.]

Lady Windermere. You will never speak against Mrs. Erlynne again, Arthur, will you?

Lord Windermere. [Gravely.] She is better than one thought her.

Lady Windermere. She is better than I am.

Lord Windermere. [Smiling as he strokes her hair.] Child, you and she belong to different worlds. Into your world evil has never entered.

Lady Windermere. Don't say that, Arthur. There is the same world for all of us, and good and evil, sin and innocence, go through it hand in hand. To shut one's eyes to half of life that one may live securely is as though one blinded oneself that one might walk with more safety in a land of pit and precipice.

Lord Windermere. [Moves down with her.] Darling, why do you say that?

Lady Windermere. [Sits on sofa.] Because I, who had shut my eyes to life, came to the brink. And one who had separated us—

Lord Windermere. We were never separated.

Lady Windermere. We never must be again. O Arthur, don't love me less, and I will trust you more. I will trust you absolutely. Let us go to Selby. In the Rose Garden at Selby the roses are white and red.

[Enter Lord Augustus C.]

Lord Augustus. Arthur, she has explained everything!

[Lady Windermere looks horribly frightened at this. Lord Windermere starts. Lord Augustus takes Windermere by the arm and brings him to front of stage. He talks rapidly and in a low voice. Lady Windermere stands watching them in terror.] My dear fellow, she has explained every demmed thing. We all wronged her immensely. It was entirely for my sake she went to Darlington's rooms. Called first at the Club—fact is, wanted to put me out of suspense—and being told I had gone on—followed—naturally frightened when she heard a lot of us coming in—retired to another room—I assure you, most gratifying to me, the whole thing. We all behaved brutally to her. She is just the woman for me. Suits me down to the ground. All the conditions she makes are that we live entirely out of England. A very good thing too. Demmed clubs, demmed climate, demmed cooks, demmed everything. Sick of it all!

Lady Windermere. [Frightened.] Has Mrs. Erlynne—?

Lord Augustus. [Advancing towards her with a low bow.] Yes, Lady Windermere— Mrs. Erlynne has done me the honour of accepting my hand.

Lord Windermere. Well, you are certainly marrying a very clever woman!

Lady Windermere. [Taking her husband's hand.] Ah, you're marrying a very good woman!

CURTAIN

About Author

Oscar Fingal O'Flahertie Wills Wilde (16 October 1854 – 30 November 1900) was an Irish poet and playwright. After writing in different forms throughout the 1880s, the early 1890s saw him become one of the most popular playwrights in London. He is best remembered for his epigrams and plays, his novel The Picture of Dorian Gray, and the circumstances of his criminal conviction for "gross indecency", imprisonment, and early death at age 46.

Wilde's parents were successful Anglo-Irish intellectuals in Dublin. A young Wilde learned to speak fluent French and German. At university, Wilde read Greats; he demonstrated himself to be an exceptional classicist, first at Trinity College Dublin, then at Oxford. He became associated with the emerging philosophy of aestheticism, led by two of his tutors, Walter Pater and John Ruskin. After university, Wilde moved to London into fashionable cultural and social circles.

As a spokesman for aestheticism, he tried his hand at various literary activities: he published a book of poems, lectured in the United States and Canada on the new "English Renaissance in Art" and interior decoration, and then returned to London where he worked prolifically as a journalist. Known for his biting wit, flamboyant dress and glittering conversational skill, Wilde became one of the best-known personalities of his day. At the turn of the 1890s, he refined his ideas about the supremacy of art in a series of dialogues and essays, and incorporated themes of decadence, duplicity, and beauty into what would be his only novel, The Picture of Dorian Gray (1890). The opportunity to construct aesthetic details precisely, and combine them with larger social themes, drew Wilde to write drama. He wrote Salome (1891) in French while in Paris but it was refused a licence for England due to an absolute prohibition on the portrayal of Biblical subjects on the English stage. Unperturbed, Wilde produced four society comedies in the early 1890s, which made him one of the most successful playwrights of late-Victorian London.

At the height of his fame and success, while The Importance of Being Earnest (1895) was still being performed in London, Wilde had the Marquess of Queensberry prosecuted for criminal libel. The Marquess was the father of Wilde's lover, Lord Alfred Douglas. The libel trial unearthed evidence that caused Wilde to drop his charges and led to his own arrest and trial for gross indecency with men. After two more trials he was convicted and sentenced to two years' hard labour, the maximum penalty, and was jailed from 1895 to 1897. During his last year in prison, he wrote De Profundis (published posthumously in 1905), a long letter which discusses his spiritual journey through his trials, forming a dark counterpoint to his earlier philosophy of pleasure. On his release, he left immediately for France, never to return to Ireland or Britain. There he wrote his last work, The Ballad of Reading Gaol (1898), a long poem commemorating the harsh rhythms of prison life.

Early life

Oscar Wilde was born at 21 Westland Row, Dublin (now home of the Oscar Wilde Centre, Trinity College), the second of three children born to Anglo-Irish Sir William Wilde and Jane Wilde, two years behind his brother William ("Willie"). Wilde's mother had distant Italian ancestry,and under the pseudonym "Speranza" (the Italian word for 'hope'), wrote poetry for the revolutionary Young Irelanders in 1848; she was a lifelong Irish nationalist. She read the Young Irelanders' poetry to Oscar and Willie, inculcating a love of these poets in her sons. Lady Wilde's interest in the neo-classical revival showed in the paintings and busts of ancient Greece and Rome in her home.

William Wilde was Ireland's leading oto-ophthalmologic (ear and eye) surgeon and was knighted in 1864 for his services as medical adviser and assistant commissioner to the censuses of Ireland. He also wrote books about Irish archaeology and peasant folklore. A renowned philanthropist, his dispensary for the care of the city's poor at the rear of Trinity College, Dublin, was the forerunner of the Dublin Eye and Ear Hospital, now located at Adelaide Road. On his father's side Wilde was descended from a Dutchman, Colonel de Wilde, who went to Ireland with King William of Orange's invading army in 1690, and numerous Anglo-Irish ancestors. On his mother's side, Wilde's ancestors included a bricklayer from County Durham, who emigrated to Ireland sometime in the 1770s.

Wilde was baptised as an infant in St. Mark's Church, Dublin, the local Church of Ireland (Anglican) church. When the church was closed, the records were moved to the nearby St. Ann's Church, Dawson Street. Davis Coakley mentions a second baptism by a Catholic priest, Father Prideaux Fox, who befriended Oscar's mother circa 1859. According to Fox's testimony in Donahoe's Magazine in 1905, Jane Wilde would visit his chapel in Glencree, County Wicklow, for Mass and would take her sons with her. She asked Father Fox in this period to baptise her sons.

Fox described it in this way:

"I am not sure if she ever became a Catholic herself but it was not long before she asked me to instruct two of her children, one of them being the future erratic genius, Oscar Wilde. After a few weeks I baptized these two children, Lady Wilde herself being present on the occasion.

In addition to his children with his wife, Sir William Wilde was the father of three children born out of wedlock before his marriage: Henry Wilson, born in 1838 to one woman, and Emily and Mary Wilde, born in 1847 and 1849, respectively, to a second woman. Sir William acknowledged paternity of his illegitimate or "natural" children and provided for their education, arranging for them to be reared by his relatives rather than with his legitimate children in his family household with his wife.

In 1855, the family moved to No. 1 Merrion Square, where Wilde's sister, Isola, was born in 1857. The Wildes' new home was larger. With both his parents' success and delight in social life, the house soon became the site of a "unique medical and cultural milieu". Guests at their salon included Sheridan Le Fanu, Charles Lever, George Petrie, Isaac Butt, William Rowan Hamilton and Samuel Ferguson.

Until he was nine, Oscar Wilde was educated at home, where a French nursemaid and a German governess taught him their languages. He attended Portora Royal School in Enniskillen, County Fermanagh, from 1864 to 1871. Until his early twenties, Wilde summered at the villa, Moytura House, which his father had built in Cong, County Mayo. There the young Wilde and his brother Willie played with George Moore.

Isola died at age nine of meningitis. Wilde's poem "Requiescat" is written to her memory.

"Tread lightly, she is near

Under the snow

Speak gently, she can hear

the daisies grow"

University education: 1870s

Trinity College, Dublin

Wilde left Portora with a royal scholarship to read classics at Trinity College, Dublin, from 1871 to 1874, sharing rooms with his older brother Willie Wilde. Trinity, one of the leading classical schools, placed him with scholars such as R. Y. Tyrell, Arthur Palmer, Edward Dowden and his tutor, Professor J. P. Mahaffy, who inspired his interest in Greek literature. As a student Wilde worked with Mahaffy on the latter's book Social Life in Greece. Wilde, despite later reservations, called Mahaffy "my first and best teacher" and "the scholar who showed me how to love Greek things".For his part, Mahaffy boasted of having created Wilde; later, he said Wilde was "the only blot on my tutorship".

The University Philosophical Society also provided an education, as members discussed intellectual and artistic subjects such as Dante Gabriel Rossetti and Algernon Charles Swinburne weekly. Wilde quickly became an established member – the members' suggestion book for 1874 contains two pages of banter (sportingly) mocking Wilde's emergent aestheticism. He presented a paper titled "Aesthetic Morality". At Trinity, Wilde established himself as an outstanding student: he came first in his class in his first year, won a scholarship by competitive examination in his second and, in his finals, won the Berkeley Gold Medal in Greek, the University's highest academic award. He was encouraged to compete for a demyship to Magdalen College, Oxford – which he won easily, having already studied Greek for over nine years.

Magdalen College, Oxford

At Magdalen, he read Greats from 1874 to 1878, and from there he applied to join the Oxford Union, but failed to be elected.

Attracted by its dress, secrecy, and ritual, Wilde petitioned the Apollo Masonic Lodge at Oxford, and was soon raised to the "Sublime Degree of Master Mason".During a resurgent interest in Freemasonry in his third year, he commented he "would be awfully sorry to give it up if I secede from the Protestant Heresy". Wilde's active involvement in Freemasonry lasted only for the time he spent at Oxford; he allowed his membership of the Apollo University Lodge to lapse after failing to pay subscriptions.

Catholicism deeply appealed to him, especially its rich liturgy, and he discussed converting to it with clergy several times. In 1877, Wilde was left speechless after an audience with Pope Pius IX in Rome.He eagerly read the books of Cardinal Newman, a noted Anglican priest who had converted to Catholicism and risen in the church hierarchy. He became more serious in 1878, when he met the Reverend Sebastian Bowden, a priest in the Brompton Oratory who had received some high-profile converts. Neither his father, who threatened to cut off his funds, nor Mahaffy thought much of the plan; but mostly Wilde, the supreme individualist, balked at the last minute from pledging himself to any formal creed. On the appointed day of his baptism, Wilde sent Father Bowden a bunch of altar lilies instead. Wilde did retain a lifelong interest in Catholic theology and liturgy.

While at Magdalen College, Wilde became particularly well known for his role in the aesthetic and decadent movements. He wore his hair long, openly scorned "manly" sports though he occasionally boxed, and he decorated his rooms with peacock feathers, lilies, sunflowers, blue china and other objets d'art. He once remarked to friends, whom he entertained lavishly, "I find it harder and harder every day to live up to my blue china." The line quickly became famous, accepted as a slogan by aesthetes but used against them by critics who sensed in it a terrible vacuousness. Some elements disdained the aesthetes, but their languishing attitudes and showy costumes became a recognised pose. Wilde was once physically attacked by a group of four fellow students, and dealt with them single-handedly, surprising critics. By his third year Wilde had truly begun to develop himself and his myth, and considered his learning to be more expansive than what was within the prescribed texts. This attitude resulted in his being rusticated for one term, after he had returned late to a college term from a trip to Greece with Mahaffy.

Wilde did not meet Walter Pater until his third year, but had been enthralled by his Studies in the History of the Renaissance, published during Wilde's final year in Trinity. Pater argued that man's sensibility to beauty should be refined above all else, and that each moment should be felt to its fullest extent. Years later, in De Profundis, Wilde described Pater's Studies... as "that book that has had such a strange influence over my life".He learned tracts of the book by heart, and carried it with him on travels in later years. Pater gave Wilde his sense of almost flippant devotion to art, though he gained a purpose for it through the lectures and writings of critic John Ruskin. Ruskin despaired at the self-validating aestheticism of Pater, arguing that the importance of art lies in its potential for the betterment of society. Ruskin admired beauty, but believed it must be allied with, and applied to, moral good. When Wilde eagerly attended Ruskin's lecture series The Aesthetic and Mathematic Schools of Art in Florence, he learned about aesthetics as the non-mathematical elements of painting. Despite being given to neither early rising nor manual labour, Wilde volunteered for Ruskin's project to convert a swampy country lane into a smart road neatly edged with flowers.

Wilde won the 1878 Newdigate Prize for his poem "Ravenna", which reflected on his visit there the year before, and he duly read it at Encaenia. In November 1878, he graduated with a double first in his B.A. of Classical Moderations and Literae Humaniores (Greats). Wilde wrote to a friend, "The dons are 'astonied' beyond words – the Bad Boy doing so well in the end!"

Apprenticeship of an aesthete: 1880s

Debut in society

After graduation from Oxford, Wilde returned to Dublin, where he met again Florence Balcombe, a childhood sweetheart. She became engaged to Bram Stoker and they married in 1878. Wilde was disappointed but stoic:

he wrote to her, remembering "the two sweet years – the sweetest years of all my youth" during which they had been close. He also stated his intention to "return to England, probably for good." This he did in 1878, only briefly visiting Ireland twice after that.

Unsure of his next step, Wilde wrote to various acquaintances enquiring about Classics positions at Oxford or Cambridge. The Rise of Historical Criticism was his submission for the Chancellor's Essay prize of 1879, which, though no longer a student, he was still eligible to enter. Its subject, "Historical Criticism among the Ancients" seemed ready-made for Wilde – with both his skill in composition and ancient learning – but he struggled to find his voice with the long, flat, scholarly style. Unusually, no prize was awarded that year.

With the last of his inheritance from the sale of his father's houses, he set himself up as a bachelor in London. The 1881 British Census listed Wilde as a boarder at 1 (now 44) Tite Street, Chelsea, where Frank Miles, a society painter, was the head of the household. Wilde spent the next six years in London and Paris, and in the United States, where he travelled to deliver lectures.

He had been publishing lyrics and poems in magazines since entering Trinity College, especially in Kottabos and the Dublin University Magazine. In mid-1881, at 27 years old, he published Poems, which collected, revised and expanded his poems.

The book was generally well received, and sold out its first print run of 750 copies. Punch was less enthusiastic, saying "The poet is Wilde, but his poetry's tame". By a tight vote, the Oxford Union condemned the book for alleged plagiarism. The librarian, who had requested the book for the library, returned the presentation copy to Wilde with a note of apology.Biographer Richard Ellmann argues that Wilde's poem "Hélas!" was a sincere, though flamboyant, attempt to explain the dichotomies the poet saw in himself; one line reads: "To drift with every passion till my soul

Is a stringed lute on which all winds can play".

The book had further printings in 1882. It was bound in a rich, enamel parchment cover (embossed with gilt blossom) and printed on hand-made Dutch paper; over the next few years, Wilde presented many copies to the dignitaries and writers who received him during his lecture tours.

America: 1882

Aestheticism was sufficiently in vogue to be caricatured by Gilbert and Sullivan in Patience (1881). Richard D'Oyly Carte, an English impresario, invited Wilde to make a lecture tour of North America, simultaneously priming the pump for the US tour of Patience and selling this most charming aesthete to the American public. Wilde journeyed on the SS Arizona, arriving 2 January 1882, and disembarking the following day. Originally planned to last four months, it continued for almost a year due to the commercial success. Wilde sought to transpose the beauty he saw in art into daily life. This was a practical as well as philosophical project: in Oxford he had surrounded himself with blue china and lilies, and now one of his lectures was on interior design.

When asked to explain reports that he had paraded down Piccadilly in London carrying a lily, long hair flowing, Wilde replied, "It's not whether I did it or not that's important, but whether people believed I did it". Wilde believed that the artist should hold forth higher ideals, and that pleasure and beauty would replace utilitarian ethics.

Wilde and aestheticism were both mercilessly caricatured and criticised in the press; the Springfield Republican, for instance, commented on Wilde's behaviour during his visit to Boston to lecture on aestheticism, suggesting that Wilde's conduct was more a bid for notoriety rather than devotion to beauty and the aesthetic. T. W. Higginson, a cleric and abolitionist, wrote in "Unmanly Manhood" of his general concern that Wilde, "whose only distinction is that he has written a thin volume of very mediocre verse", would improperly influence the behaviour of men and women.

According to biographer Michèle Mendelssohn, Wilde was the subject of anti-Irish caricature and was portrayed as a monkey, a blackface performer and a Christy's Minstrel throughout his career."Harper's Weekly put a sunflower-worshipping monkey dressed as Wilde on the front of the January 1882 issue. The magazine didn't let its reputation for quality impede its expression of what are now considered odious ethnic and racial ideologies. The drawing stimulated other American maligners and, in England, had a full-page reprint in the Lady's Pictorial. ... When the National Republican discussed Wilde, it was to explain 'a few items as to the animal's pedigree.' And on 22 January 1882 the Washington Post illustrated the Wild Man of Borneo alongside Oscar Wilde of England and asked 'How far is it from this to this?' "Though his press reception was hostile, Wilde was well received in diverse settings across America; he drank whiskey with miners in Leadville, Colorado, and was fêted at the most fashionable salons in many cities he visited.

London life and marriage

His earnings, plus expected income from The Duchess of Padua, allowed him to move to Paris between February and mid-May 1883. While there he met Robert Sherard, whom he entertained constantly. "We are dining on the Duchess tonight", Wilde would declare before taking him to an expensive restaurant. In August he briefly returned to New York for the production of Vera, his first play, after it was turned down in London. He reportedly entertained the other passengers with "Ave Imperatrix!, A Poem on England", about the rise and fall of empires. E. C. Stedman, in Victorian Poets, describes this "lyric to England" as "manly verse – a poetic and eloquent invocation". The play was initially well received by the audience, but when the critics wrote lukewarm reviews, attendance fell sharply and the play closed a week after it had opened.

Wilde had to return to England, where he continued to lecture on topics including Personal Impressions of America, The Value of Art in Modern Life, and Dress.

In London, he had been introduced in 1881 to Constance Lloyd, daughter of Horace Lloyd, a wealthy Queen's Counsel, and his wife. She happened to be visiting Dublin in 1884, when Wilde was lecturing at the Gaiety Theatre. He proposed to her, and they married on 29 May 1884 at the Anglican St James's Church, Paddington, in London. Although Constance had an annual allowance of £250, which was generous for a young woman (equivalent to about £25,600 in current value), the Wildes had relatively luxurious tastes. They had preached to others for so long on the subject of design that people expected their home to set new standards. No. 16, Tite Street was duly renovated in seven months at considerable expense. The couple had two sons together, Cyril (1885) and Vyvyan (1886). Wilde became the sole literary signatory of George Bernard Shaw's petition for a pardon of the anarchists arrested (and later executed) after the Haymarket massacre in Chicago in 1886.

Robert Ross had read Wilde's poems before they met at Oxford in 1886. He seemed unrestrained by the Victorian prohibition against homosexuality, and became estranged from his family. By Richard Ellmann's account, he was a precocious seventeen-year-old who "so young and yet so knowing, was determined to seduce Wilde". According to Daniel Mendelsohn, Wilde, who had long alluded to Greek love, was "initiated into homosexual sex" by Ross, while his "marriage had begun to unravel after his wife's second pregnancy, which left him physically repelled".

Prose writing: 1886–91

Journalism and editorship: 1886–89

Criticism over artistic matters in The Pall Mall Gazette provoked a letter in self-defence, and soon Wilde was a contributor to that and other journals during 1885–87. He enjoyed reviewing and journalism; the form suited his style. He could organise and share his views on art, literature and life, yet in a format less tedious than lecturing. Buoyed up, his reviews were largely chatty and positive. Wilde, like his parents before him, also supported the cause of Irish nationalism. When Charles Stewart Parnell was falsely accused of inciting murder, Wilde wrote a series of astute columns defending him in the Daily Chronicle.

His flair, having previously been put mainly into socialising, suited journalism and rapidly attracted notice. With his youth nearly over, and a family to support, in mid-1887 Wilde became the editor of The Lady's World magazine, his name prominently appearing on the cover. He promptly renamed it as The Woman's World and raised its tone, adding serious articles on parenting, culture, and politics, while keeping discussions of fashion and arts. Two pieces of fiction were usually included, one to be read to children, the other for the ladies themselves. Wilde worked hard to solicit good contributions from his wide artistic acquaintance, including those of Lady Wilde and his wife Constance, while his own "Literary and Other Notes" were themselves popular and amusing.

The initial vigour and excitement which he brought to the job began to fade as administration, commuting and office life became tedious. At the same time as Wilde's interest flagged, the publishers became concerned anew about circulation: sales, at the relatively high price of one shilling, remained low. Increasingly sending instructions to the magazine by letter, Wilde began a new period of creative work and his own column appeared less regularly.In October 1889, Wilde had finally found his voice in prose and, at the end of the second volume, Wilde left The Woman's World. The magazine outlasted him by one issue.

If Wilde's period at the helm of the magazine was a mixed success from an organizational point of view, it played a pivotal role in his development as a writer and facilitated his ascent to fame. Whilst Wilde the journalist supplied articles under the guidance of his editors, Wilde the editor was forced to learn to manipulate the literary marketplace on his own terms.

During the late 1880s, Wilde was a close friend of the artist James NcNeill Whistler and they dined together on many occasions. At one of these dinners, Whistler said a bon mot that Wilde found particularly witty, Wilde exclaimed that he wished that he had said it, and Whistler retorted "You will, Oscar, you will".Herbert Vivian—a mutual friend of Wilde and Whistler—attended the dinner and recorded it in his article The Reminiscences of a Short Life which appeared in The Sun in 1889. The article alleged that Wilde had a habit of passing off other people's witticisms as his own—especially Whistler's. Wilde considered Vivian's article to be a scurrilous betrayal, and it directly caused the broken friendship between Wilde and Whistler. The Reminiscences also caused great acrimony between Wilde and Vivian, Wilde accusing Vivian of "the inaccuracy of an eavesdropper with the method of a blackmailer" and banishing Vivian from his circle.

Shorter fiction

Wilde published The Happy Prince and Other Tales in 1888, and had been regularly writing fairy stories for magazines. In 1891 he published two more collections, Lord Arthur Savile's Crime and Other Stories, and in September A House of Pomegranates was dedicated "To Constance Mary Wilde". "The Portrait of Mr. W. H.", which Wilde had begun in 1887, was first published in Blackwood's Edinburgh Magazine in July 1889. It is a short story, which reports a conversation, in which the theory that Shakespeare's sonnets were written out of the poet's love of the boy actor "Willie Hughes", is advanced, retracted, and then propounded again. The only evidence for this is two supposed puns within the sonnets themselves.

The anonymous narrator is at first sceptical, then believing, finally flirtatious with the reader: he concludes that "there is really a great deal to be said of the Willie Hughes theory of Shakespeare's sonnets." By the end fact and fiction have melded together. Arthur Ransome wrote that Wilde "read something of himself into Shakespeare's sonnets" and became fascinated with the "Willie Hughes theory" despite the lack of biographical evidence for the historical William Hughes' existence. Instead of writing a short but serious essay on the question, Wilde tossed the theory amongst the three characters of the story, allowing it to unfold as background to the plot. The story thus is an early masterpiece of Wilde's combining many elements that interested him: conversation, literature and the idea that to shed oneself of an idea one must first convince another of its truth. Ransome concludes that Wilde succeeds precisely because the literary criticism is unveiled with such a deft touch.

Though containing nothing but "special pleading", it would not, he says "be possible to build an airier castle in Spain than this of the imaginary William Hughes" we continue listening nonetheless to be charmed by the telling. "You must believe in Willie Hughes," Wilde told an acquaintance, "I almost do, myself."

Essays and dialogues

Wilde, having tired of journalism, had been busy setting out his aesthetic ideas more fully in a series of longer prose pieces which were published in the major literary-intellectual journals of the day. In January 1889, The Decay of Lying: A Dialogue appeared in The Nineteenth Century, and Pen, Pencil and Poison, a satirical biography of Thomas Griffiths Wainewright, in The Fortnightly Review, edited by Wilde's friend Frank Harris. Two of Wilde's four writings on aesthetics are dialogues: though Wilde had evolved professionally from lecturer to writer, he retained an oral tradition of sorts. Having always excelled as a wit and raconteur, he often composed by assembling phrases, bons mots and witticisms into a longer, cohesive work.

Wilde was concerned about the effect of moralising on art; he believed in art's redemptive, developmental powers: "Art is individualism, and individualism is a disturbing and disintegrating force. There lies its immense value. For what it seeks is to disturb monotony of type, slavery of custom, tyranny of habit, and the reduction of man to the level of a machine." In his only political text, The Soul of Man Under Socialism, he argued political conditions should establish this primacy – private property should be abolished, and cooperation should be substituted for competition. At the same time, he stressed that the government most amenable to artists was no government at all. Wilde envisioned a society where mechanisation has freed human effort from the burden of necessity, effort which can instead be expended on artistic creation. George Orwell summarised, "In effect, the world will be populated by artists, each striving after perfection in the way that seems best to him."

This point of view did not align him with the Fabians, intellectual socialists who advocated using state apparatus to change social conditions, nor did it endear him to the monied classes whom he had previously entertained. Hesketh Pearson, introducing a collection of Wilde's essays in 1950, remarked how The Soul of Man Under Socialism had been an inspirational text for revolutionaries in Tsarist Russia but laments that in the Stalinist era "it is doubtful whether there are any uninspected places in which it could now be hidden".

Wilde considered including this pamphlet and The Portrait of Mr. W.H., his essay-story on Shakespeare's sonnets, in a new anthology in 1891, but eventually decided to limit it to purely aesthetic subjects. Intentions packaged revisions of four essays: The Decay of Lying, Pen, Pencil and Poison, The Truth of Masks (first published 1885), and The Critic as Artist in two parts. For Pearson the biographer, the essays and dialogues exhibit every aspect of Wilde's genius and character: wit, romancer, talker, lecturer, humanist and scholar and concludes that "no other productions of his have as varied an appeal". 1891 turned out to be Wilde's annus mirabilis; apart from his three collections he also produced his only novel.

The Picture of Dorian Gray

The first version of The Picture of Dorian Gray was published as the lead story in the July 1890 edition of Lippincott's Monthly Magazine, along with five others. The story begins with a man painting a picture of Gray. When Gray, who has a "face like ivory and rose leaves", sees his finished portrait, he breaks down. Distraught that his beauty will fade while the portrait stays beautiful, he inadvertently makes a Faustian bargain in which only the painted image grows old while he stays beautiful and young. For Wilde, the purpose of art would be to guide life as if beauty alone were its object. As Gray's portrait allows him to escape the corporeal ravages of his hedonism, Wilde sought to juxtapose the beauty he saw in art with daily life.

Reviewers immediately criticised the novel's decadence and homosexual allusions; The Daily Chronicle for example, called it "unclean", "poisonous", and "heavy with the mephitic odours of moral and spiritual putrefaction". Which he clarified his stance on ethics and aesthetics in art – "If a work of art is rich and vital and complete, those who have artistic instincts will see its beauty and those to whom ethics appeal more strongly will see its moral lesson." He nevertheless revised it extensively for book publication in 1891: six new chapters were added, some overtly decadent passages and homo-eroticism excised, and a preface was included consisting of twenty two epigrams, such as "Books are well written, or badly written. That is all."

Contemporary reviewers and modern critics have postulated numerous possible sources of the story, a search Jershua McCormack argues is futile because Wilde "has tapped a root of Western folklore so deep and ubiquitous that the story has escaped its origins and returned to the oral tradition." Wilde claimed the plot was "an idea that is as old as the history of literature but to which I have given a new form".Modern critic Robin McKie considered the novel to be technically mediocre, saying that the conceit of the plot had guaranteed its fame, but the device is never pushed to its full.On the other hand, Robert McCrum of The Guardian deemed it the 27th best novel ever written in English, calling it "an arresting, and slightly camp, exercise in late-Victorian gothic."

Theatrical career: 1892–95

Salomé

The 1891 census records the Wildes' residence at 16 Tite Street, where he lived with his wife Constance and two sons. Wilde though, not content with being better known than ever in London, returned to Paris in October 1891, this time as a respected writer. He was received at the salons littéraires, including the famous mardis of Stéphane Mallarmé, a renowned symbolist poet of the time. Wilde's two plays during the 1880s, Vera; or, The Nihilists and The Duchess of Padua, had not met with much success. He had continued his interest in the theatre and now, after finding his voice in prose, his thoughts turned again to the dramatic form as the biblical iconography of Salome filled his mind. One evening, after discussing depictions of Salome throughout history, he returned to his hotel and noticed a blank copybook lying on the desk, and it occurred to him to write in it what he had been saying. The result was a new play, Salomé, written rapidly and in French.

A tragedy, it tells the story of Salome, the stepdaughter of the tetrarch Herod Antipas, who, to her stepfather's dismay but mother's delight, requests the head of Jokanaan (John the Baptist) on a silver platter as a reward for dancing the Dance of the Seven Veils. When Wilde returned to London just before Christmas the Paris Echo referred to him as "le great event" of the season. Rehearsals of the play, starring Sarah Bernhardt, began but the play was refused a licence by the Lord Chamberlain, since it depicted biblical characters. Salome was published jointly in Paris and London in 1893, but was not performed until 1896 in Paris, during Wilde's later incarceration.

Comedies of society

Wilde, who had first set out to irritate Victorian society with his dress and talking points, then outrage it with Dorian Gray, his novel of vice hidden beneath art, finally found a way to critique society on its own terms. Lady Windermere's Fan was first performed on 20 February 1892 at St James's Theatre, packed with the cream of society. On the surface a witty comedy, there is subtle subversion underneath: "it concludes with collusive concealment rather than collective disclosure". The audience, like Lady Windermere, are forced to soften harsh social codes in favour of a more nuanced view. The play was enormously popular, touring the country for months, but largely trashed by conservative critics. It was followed by A Woman of No Importance in 1893, another Victorian comedy, revolving around the spectre of illegitimate births, mistaken identities and late revelations. Wilde was commissioned to write two more plays and An Ideal Husband, written in 1894, followed in January 1895.

Peter Raby said these essentially English plays were well-pitched, "Wilde, with one eye on the dramatic genius of Ibsen, and the other on the commercial competition in London's West End, targeted his audience with adroit precision".

Queensberry family

In mid-1891 Lionel Johnson introduced Wilde to Lord Alfred Douglas, Johnson's cousin and an undergraduate at Oxford at the time. Known to his family and friends as "Bosie", he was a handsome and spoilt young man. An intimate friendship sprang up between Wilde and Douglas and by 1893 Wilde was infatuated with Douglas and they consorted together regularly in a tempestuous affair. If Wilde was relatively indiscreet, even flamboyant, in the way he acted, Douglas was reckless in public. Wilde, who was earning up to £100 a week from his plays (his salary at The Woman's World had been £6), indulged Douglas's every whim: material, artistic or sexual.

Douglas soon initiated Wilde into the Victorian underground of gay prostitution and Wilde was introduced to a series of young working-class male prostitutes from 1892 onwards by Alfred Taylor. These infrequent rendezvous usually took the same form: Wilde would meet the boy, offer him gifts, dine him privately and then take him to a hotel room. Unlike Wilde's idealised relations with Ross, John Gray, and Douglas, all of whom remained part of his aesthetic circle, these consorts were uneducated and knew nothing of literature. Soon his public and private lives had become sharply divided; in De Profundis he wrote to Douglas that "It was like feasting with panthers; the danger was half the excitement... I did not know that when they were to strike at me it was to be at another's piping and at another's pay."

Douglas and some Oxford friends founded a journal, The Chameleon, to which Wilde "sent a page of paradoxes originally destined for the Saturday Review". "Phrases and Philosophies for the Use of the Young" was to come under attack six months later at Wilde's trial, where he was forced to defend the magazine to which he had sent his work.In any case, it became unique: The Chameleon was not published again.

Lord Alfred's father, the Marquess of Queensberry, was known for his outspoken atheism, brutish manner and creation of the modern rules of boxing. Queensberry, who feuded regularly with his son, confronted Wilde and Lord Alfred about the nature of their relationship several times, but Wilde was able to mollify him. In June 1894, he called on Wilde at 16 Tite Street, without an appointment, and clarified his stance: "I do not say that you are it, but you look it, and pose at it, which is just as bad. And if I catch you and my son again in any public restaurant I will thrash you" to which Wilde responded: "I don't know what the Queensberry rules are, but the Oscar Wilde rule is to shoot on sight".His account in De Profundis was less triumphant: "It was when, in my library at Tite Street, waving his small hands in the air in epileptic fury, your father... stood uttering every foul word his foul mind could think of, and screaming the loathsome threats he afterwards with such cunning carried out". Queensberry only described the scene once, saying Wilde had "shown him the white feather", meaning he had acted in a cowardly way. Though trying to remain calm, Wilde saw that he was becoming ensnared in a brutal family quarrel. He did not wish to bear Queensberry's insults, but he knew to confront him could lead to disaster were his liaisons disclosed publicly.

The Importance of Being Earnest

Wilde's final play again returns to the theme of switched identities: the play's two protagonists engage in "bunburying" (the maintenance of alternative personas in the town and country) which allows them to escape Victorian social mores.Earnest is even lighter in tone than Wilde's earlier comedies. While their characters often rise to serious themes in moments of crisis, Earnest lacks the by-now stock Wildean characters: there is no "woman with a past", the principals are neither villainous nor cunning, simply idle cultivés, and the idealistic young women are not that innocent. Mostly set in drawing rooms and almost completely lacking in action or violence, Earnest lacks the self-conscious decadence found in The Picture of Dorian Gray and Salome.

The play, now considered Wilde's masterpiece, was rapidly written in Wilde's artistic maturity in late 1894. It was first performed on 14 February 1895, at St James's Theatre in London, Wilde's second collaboration with George Alexander, the actor-manager. Both author and producer assiduously revised, prepared and rehearsed every line, scene and setting in the months before the premiere, creating a carefully constructed representation of late-Victorian society, yet simultaneously mocking it. During rehearsal Alexander requested that Wilde shorten the play from four acts to three, which the author did. Premieres at St James's seemed like "brilliant parties", and the opening of The Importance of Being Earnest was no exception. Allan Aynesworth (who played Algernon) recalled to Hesketh Pearson, "In my fifty-three years of acting, I never remember a greater triumph than [that] first night."Earnest's immediate reception as Wilde's best work to date finally crystallised his fame into a solid artistic reputation. The Importance of Being Earnest remains his most popular play.

Wilde's professional success was mirrored by an escalation in his feud with Queensberry. Queensberry had planned to insult Wilde publicly by throwing a bouquet of rotting vegetables onto the stage; Wilde was tipped off and had Queensberry barred from entering the theatre.Fifteen weeks later Wilde was in prison.

Trials

Wilde v. Queensberry

On 18 February 1895, the Marquess left his calling card at Wilde's club, the Albemarle, inscribed: "For Oscar Wilde, posing somdomite" Wilde, encouraged by Douglas and against the advice of his friends, initiated a private prosecution against Queensberry for libel, since the note amounted to a public accusation that Wilde had committed the crime of sodomy.

Queensberry was arrested for criminal libel; a charge carrying a possible sentence of up to two years in prison. Under the 1843 Libel Act, Queensberry could avoid conviction for libel only by demonstrating that his accusation was in fact true, and furthermore that there was some "public benefit" to having made the accusation openly. Queensberry's lawyers thus hired private detectives to find evidence of Wilde's homosexual liaisons.

Wilde's friends had advised him against the prosecution at a Saturday Review meeting at the Café Royal on 24 March 1895; Frank Harris warned him that "they are going to prove sodomy against you" and advised him to flee to France. Wilde and Douglas walked out in a huff, Wilde saying "it is at such moments as these that one sees who are one's true friends". The scene was witnessed by George Bernard Shaw who recalled it to Arthur Ransome a day or so before Ransome's trial for libelling Douglas in 1913. To Ransome it confirmed what he had said in his 1912 book on Wilde; that Douglas's rivalry for Wilde with Robbie Ross and his arguments with his father had resulted in Wilde's public disaster; as Wilde wrote in De Profundis. Douglas lost his case. Shaw included an account of the argument between Harris, Douglas and Wilde in the preface to his play The Dark Lady of the Sonnets.

The libel trial became a cause célèbre as salacious details of Wilde's private life with Taylor and Douglas began to appear in the press. A team of private detectives had directed Queensberry's lawyers, led by Edward Carson QC, to the world of the Victorian underground. Wilde's association with blackmailers and male prostitutes, cross-dressers and homosexual brothels was recorded, and various persons involved were interviewed, some being coerced to appear as witnesses since they too were accomplices to the crimes of which Wilde was accused.

The trial opened on 3 April 1895 before Justice Richard Henn Collins amid scenes of near hysteria both in the press and the public galleries. The extent of the evidence massed against Wilde forced him to declare meekly, "I am the prosecutor in this case"Wilde's lawyer, Sir Edward George Clarke, opened the case by pre-emptively asking Wilde about two suggestive letters Wilde had written to Douglas, which the defence had in its possession. He characterised the first as a "prose sonnet" and admitted that the "poetical language" might seem strange to the court but claimed its intent was innocent. Wilde stated that the letters had been obtained by blackmailers who had attempted to extort money from him, but he had refused, suggesting they should take the £60 (equal to £6,800 today) offered, "unusual for a prose piece of that length". He claimed to regard the letters as works of art rather than something of which to be ashamed.

Carson, a fellow Dubliner who had attended Trinity College, Dublin at the same time as Wilde, cross-examined Wilde on how he perceived the moral content of his works. Wilde replied with characteristic wit and flippancy, claiming that works of art are not capable of being moral or immoral but only well or poorly made, and that only "brutes and illiterates", whose views on art "are incalculably stupid", would make such judgements about art. Carson, a leading barrister, diverged from the normal practice of asking closed questions. Carson pressed Wilde on each topic from every angle, squeezing out nuances of meaning from Wilde's answers, removing them from their aesthetic context and portraying Wilde as evasive and decadent. While Wilde won the most laughs from the court, Carson scored the most legal points. To undermine Wilde's credibility, and to justify Queensberry's description of Wilde as a "posing somdomite", Carson drew from the witness an admission of his capacity for "posing", by demonstrating that he had lied about his age on oath. Playing on this, he returned to the topic throughout his cross-examination. Carson also tried to justify Queensberry's characterisation by quoting from Wilde's novel, The Picture of Dorian Gray, referring in particular to a scene in the second chapter, in which Lord Henry Wotton explains his decadent philosophy to Dorian, an "innocent young man", in Carson's words.

Carson then moved to the factual evidence and questioned Wilde about his friendships with younger, lower-class men. Wilde admitted being on a first-name basis and lavishing gifts upon them, but insisted that nothing untoward had occurred and that the men were merely good friends of his. Carson repeatedly pointed out the unusual nature of these relationships and insinuated that the men were prostitutes. Wilde replied that he did not believe in social barriers, and simply enjoyed the society of young men. Then Carson asked Wilde directly whether he had ever kissed a certain servant boy, Wilde responded, "Oh, dear no. He was a particularly plain boy – unfortunately ugly – I pitied him for it." Carson pressed him on the answer, repeatedly asking why the boy's ugliness was relevant. Wilde hesitated, then for the first time became flustered: "You sting me and insult me and try to unnerve me; and at times one says things flippantly when one ought to speak more seriously."

In his opening speech for the defence, Carson announced that he had located several male prostitutes who were to testify that they had had sex with Wilde. On the advice of his lawyers, Wilde dropped the prosecution. Queensberry was found not guilty, as the court declared that his accusation that Wilde was "posing as a Somdomite " was justified, "true in substance and in fact".Under the Libel Act 1843, Queensberry's acquittal rendered Wilde legally liable for the considerable expenses Queensberry had incurred in his defence, which left Wilde bankrupt.

Regina v. Wilde

After Wilde left the court, a warrant for his arrest was applied for on charges of sodomy and gross indecency. Robbie Ross found Wilde at the Cadogan Hotel, Pont Street, Knightsbridge, with Reginald Turner; both men advised Wilde to go at once to Dover and try to get a boat to France; his mother advised him to stay and fight. Wilde, lapsing into inaction, could only say, "The train has gone. It's too late."On 6 April 1895, Wilde was arrested for "gross indecency" under Section 11 of the Criminal Law Amendment Act 1885, a term meaning homosexual acts not amounting to buggery (an offence under a separate statute). At Wilde's instruction, Ross and Wilde's butler forced their way into the bedroom and library of 16 Tite Street, packing some personal effects, manuscripts, and letters. Wilde was then imprisoned on remand at Holloway, where he received daily visits from Douglas.

Events moved quickly and his prosecution opened on 26 April 1895, before Mr Justice Charles. Wilde pleaded not guilty. He had already begged Douglas to leave London for Paris, but Douglas complained bitterly, even wanting to give evidence; he was pressed to go and soon fled to the Hotel du Monde. Fearing persecution, Ross and many others also left the United Kingdom during this time. Under cross examination Wilde was at first hesitant, then spoke eloquently:

Charles Gill (prosecuting): What is "the love that dare not speak its name"?

Wilde: "The love that dare not speak its name" in this century is such a great affection of an elder for a younger man as there was between David and Jonathan, such as Plato made the very basis of his philosophy, and such as you find in the sonnets of Michelangelo and Shakespeare. It is that deep spiritual affection that is as pure as it is perfect. It dictates and pervades great works of art, like those of Shakespeare and Michelangelo, and those two letters of mine, such as they are. It is in this century misunderstood, so much misunderstood that it may be described as "the love that dare not speak its name", and on that account of it I am placed where I am now. It is beautiful, it is fine, it is the noblest form of affection. There is nothing unnatural about it. It is intellectual, and it repeatedly exists between an older and a younger man, when the older man has intellect, and the younger man has all the joy, hope and glamour of life before him. That it should be so, the world does not understand. The world mocks at it, and sometimes puts one in the pillory for it.

This response was counter-productive in a legal sense as it only served to reinforce the charges of homosexual behaviour.

The trial ended with the jury unable to reach a verdict. Wilde's counsel, Sir Edward Clarke, was finally able to get a magistrate to allow Wilde and his friends to post bail. The Reverend Stewart Headlam put up most of the £5,000 surety required by the court, having disagreed with Wilde's treatment by the press and the courts. Wilde was freed from Holloway and, shunning attention, went into hiding at the house of Ernest and Ada Leverson, two of his firm friends. Edward Carson approached Frank Lockwood QC, the Solicitor General and asked "Can we not let up on the fellow now?" Lockwood answered that he would like to do so, but feared that the case had become too politicised to be dropped.

The final trial was presided over by Mr Justice Wills. On 25 May 1895 Wilde and Alfred Taylor were convicted of gross indecency and sentenced to two years' hard labour. The judge described the sentence, the maximum allowed, as "totally inadequate for a case such as this", and that the case was "the worst case I have ever tried". Wilde's response "And I? May I say nothing, my Lord?" was drowned out in cries of "Shame" in the courtroom.

Imprisonment

When first I was put into prison some people advised me to try and forget who I was. It was ruinous advice. It is only by realising what I am that I have found comfort of any kind. Now I am advised by others to try on my release to forget that I have ever been in a prison at all. I know that would be equally fatal. It would mean that I would always be haunted by an intolerable sense of disgrace, and that those things that are meant for me as much as for anybody else – the beauty of the sun and moon, the pageant of the seasons, the music of daybreak and the silence of great nights, the rain falling through the leaves, or the dew creeping over the grass and making it silver – would all be tainted for me, and lose their healing power, and their power of communicating joy. To regret one's own experiences is to arrest one's own development. To deny one's own experiences is to put a lie into the lips of one's own life. It is no less than a denial of the soul.

De Profundis

Wilde was incarcerated from 25 May 1895 to 18 May 1897.

He first entered Newgate Prison in London for processing, then was moved to Pentonville Prison, where the "hard labour" to which he had been sentenced consisted of many hours of walking a treadmill and picking oakum (separating the fibres in scraps of old navy ropes), and where prisoners were allowed to read only the Bible and The Pilgrim's Progress.

A few months later he was moved to Wandsworth Prison in London. Inmates there also followed the regimen of "hard labour, hard fare and a hard bed", which wore harshly on Wilde's delicate health. In November he collapsed during chapel from illness and hunger. His right ear drum was ruptured in the fall, an injury that later contributed to his death. He spent two months in the infirmary.

Richard B. Haldane, the Liberal MP and reformer, visited Wilde and had him transferred in November to Reading Gaol, 30 miles (48 km) west of London on 23 November 1895. The transfer itself was the lowest point of his incarceration, as a crowd jeered and spat at him on the railway platform. He spent the remainder of his sentence there, addressed and identified only as "C33" – the occupant of the third cell on the third floor of C ward.

About five months after Wilde arrived at Reading Gaol, Charles Thomas Wooldridge, a trooper in the Royal Horse Guards, was brought to Reading to await his trial for murdering his wife on 29 March 1896; on 17 June Wooldridge was sentenced to death and returned to Reading for his execution, which took place on Tuesday, 7 July 1896 – the first hanging at Reading in 18 years. From Wooldridge's hanging, Wilde later wrote The Ballad of Reading Gaol.

Wilde was not, at first, even allowed paper and pen but Haldane eventually succeeded in allowing access to books and writing materials. Wilde requested, among others: the Bible in French; Italian and German grammars; some Ancient Greek texts, Dante's Divine Comedy, Joris-Karl Huysmans's new French novel about Christian redemption En route, and essays by St Augustine, Cardinal Newman and Walter Pater.

Between January and March 1897 Wilde wrote a 50,000-word letter to Douglas. He was not allowed to send it, but was permitted to take it with him when released from prison. In reflective mode, Wilde coldly examines his career to date, how he had been a colourful agent provocateur in Victorian society, his art, like his paradoxes, seeking to subvert as well as sparkle. His own estimation of himself was: one who "stood in symbolic relations to the art and culture of my age". It was from these heights that his life with Douglas began, and Wilde examines that particularly closely, repudiating him for what Wilde finally sees as his arrogance and vanity: he had not forgotten Douglas' remark, when he was ill, "When you are not on your pedestal you are not interesting." Wilde blamed himself, though, for the ethical degradation of character that he allowed Douglas to bring about in him and took responsibility for his own fall, "I am here for having tried to put your father in prison." The first half concludes with Wilde forgiving Douglas, for his own sake as much as Douglas's. The second half of the letter traces Wilde's spiritual journey of redemption and fulfilment through his prison reading. He realised that his ordeal had filled his soul with the fruit of experience, however bitter it tasted at the time.

> ... I wanted to eat of the fruit of all the trees in the garden of the world ... And so, indeed, I went out, and so I lived. My only mistake was that I confined myself so exclusively to the trees of what seemed to me the sun-lit side of the garden, and shunned the other side for its shadow and its gloom.

Wilde was released from prison on 19 May 1897 and sailed that evening for Dieppe, France. He never returned to the UK.

On his release, he gave the manuscript to Ross, who may or may not have carried out Wilde's instructions to send a copy to Douglas (who later denied having received it). The letter was partially published in 1905 as De Profundis; its complete and correct publication first occurred in 1962 in The Letters of Oscar Wilde.

Decline: 1897–1900

Exile

Though Wilde's health had suffered greatly from the harshness and diet of prison, he had a feeling of spiritual renewal. He immediately wrote to the Society of Jesus requesting a six-month Catholic retreat; when the request was denied, Wilde wept. "I intend to be received into the Catholic Church before long", Wilde told a journalist who asked about his religious intentions.

He spent his last three years impoverished and in exile. He took the name "Sebastian Melmoth", after Saint Sebastian and the titular character of Melmoth the Wanderer (a Gothic novel by Charles Maturin, Wilde's great-uncle). Wilde wrote two long letters to the editor of the Daily Chronicle, describing the brutal conditions of English prisons and advocating penal reform. His discussion of the dismissal of Warder Martin for giving biscuits to an anaemic child prisoner repeated the themes of the corruption and degeneration of punishment that he had earlier outlined in The Soul of Man under Socialism.

Wilde spent mid-1897 with Robert Ross in the seaside village of Berneval-le-Grand in northern France, where he wrote The Ballad of Reading Gaol, narrating the execution of Charles Thomas Wooldridge, who murdered his wife in a rage at her infidelity. It moves from an objective story-telling to symbolic identification with the prisoners. No attempt is made to assess the justice of the laws which convicted them but rather the poem highlights the brutalisation of the punishment that all convicts share. Wilde juxtaposes the executed man and himself with the line "Yet each man kills the thing he loves". He adopted the proletarian ballad form and the author was credited as "C33", Wilde's cell number in Reading Gaol. He suggested that it be published in Reynolds' Magazine, "because it circulates widely among the criminal classes – to which I now belong – for once I will be read by my peers – a new experience for me". It was an immediate roaring commercial success, going through seven editions in less than two years, only after which "[Oscar" was added to the title page, though many in literary circles had known Wilde to be the author. It brought him a small amount of money.

Although Douglas had been the cause of his misfortunes, he and Wilde were reunited in August 1897 at Rouen. This meeting was disapproved of by the friends and families of both men. Constance Wilde was already refusing to meet Wilde or allow him to see their sons, though she sent him money – three pounds a week. During the latter part of 1897, Wilde and Douglas lived together near Naples for a few months until they were separated by their families under the threat of cutting off all funds.

Wilde's final address was at the dingy Hôtel d'Alsace (now known as L'Hôtel), on rue des Beaux-Arts in Saint-Germain-des-Prés, Paris. "This poverty really breaks one's heart: it is so sale , so utterly depressing, so hopeless. Pray do what you can" he wrote to his publisher. He corrected and published An Ideal Husband and The Importance of Being Earnest, the proofs of which, according to Ellmann, show a man "very much in command of himself and of the play" but he refused to write anything else: "I can write, but have lost the joy of writing".

He wandered the boulevards alone and spent what little money he had on alcohol. A series of embarrassing chance encounters with hostile English visitors, or Frenchmen he had known in better days, drowned his spirit. Soon Wilde was sufficiently confined to his hotel to joke, on one of his final trips outside, "My wallpaper and I are fighting a duel to the death. One of us has got to go". On 12 October 1900 he sent a telegram to Ross: "Terribly weak. Please come". His moods fluctuated; Max Beerbohm relates how their mutual friend Reginald 'Reggie' Turner had found Wilde very depressed after a nightmare. "I dreamt that I had died, and was supping with the dead!" "I am sure", Turner replied, "that you must have been the life and soul of the party." Turner was one of the few of the old circle who remained with Wilde to the end and was at his bedside when he died.

Death

By 25 November 1900 Wilde had developed meningitis, then called "cerebral meningitis". Robbie Ross arrived on 29 November, sent for a priest, and Wilde was conditionally baptised into the Catholic Church by Fr Cuthbert Dunne, a Passionist priest from Dublin, Wilde having been baptised in the Church of Ireland and having moreover a recollection of Catholic baptism as a child, a fact later attested to by the minister of the sacrament, Fr Lawrence Fox. Fr Dunne recorded the baptism,

As the voiture rolled through the dark streets that wintry night, the sad story of Oscar Wilde was in part repeated to me... Robert Ross knelt by the bedside, assisting me as best he could while I administered conditional baptism, and afterwards answering the responses while I gave Extreme Unction to the prostrate man and recited the prayers for the dying. As the man was in a semi-comatose condition, I did not venture to administer the Holy Viaticum; still I must add that he could be roused and was roused from this state in my presence. When roused, he gave signs of being inwardly conscious... Indeed I was fully satisfied that he understood me when told that I was about to receive him into the Catholic Church and gave him the Last Sacraments... And when I repeated close to his ear the Holy Names, the Acts of Contrition, Faith, Hope and Charity, with acts of humble resignation to the Will of God, he tried all through to say the words after me.

Wilde died of meningitis on 30 November 1900. Different opinions are given as to the cause of the disease: Richard Ellmann claimed it was syphilitic; Merlin Holland, Wilde's grandson, thought this to be a misconception, noting that Wilde's meningitis followed a surgical intervention, perhaps a mastoidectomy; Wilde's physicians, Dr Paul Cleiss and A'Court Tucker, reported that the condition stemmed from an old suppuration of the right ear (from the prison injury, see above) treated for several years (une ancienne suppuration de l'oreille droite d'ailleurs en traitement depuis plusieurs années) and made no allusion to syphilis.

Burial

Wilde was initially buried in the Cimetière de Bagneux outside Paris; in 1909 his remains were disinterred and transferred to Père Lachaise Cemetery, inside the city. His tomb there was designed by Sir Jacob Epstein. It was commissioned by Robert Ross, who asked for a small compartment to be made for his own ashes, which were duly transferred in 1950. The modernist angel depicted as a relief on the tomb was originally complete with male genitalia, which were initially censored by French Authorities with a golden leaf. The genitals have since been vandalised; their current whereabouts are unknown. In 2000, Leon Johnson, a multimedia artist, installed a silver prosthesis to replace them. In 2011, the tomb was cleaned of the many lipstick marks left there by admirers and a glass barrier was installed to prevent further marks or damage.

The epitaph is a verse from The Ballad of Reading Gaol,

And alien tears will fill for him

Pity's long-broken urn,

For his mourners will be outcast men,

And outcasts always mourn.

Posthumous pardon

In 2017, Wilde was among an estimated 50,000 men who were pardoned for homosexual acts that were no longer considered offences under the Policing and Crime Act 2017. The Act is known informally as the Alan Turing law.

Honours

In 2014 Wilde was one of the inaugural honorees in the Rainbow Honor Walk, a walk of fame in San Francisco's Castro neighbourhood noting LGBTQ people who have "made significant contributions in their fields."

Biographies

Wilde's life has been the subject of numerous biographies since his death. The earliest were memoirs by those who knew him: often they are personal or impressionistic accounts which can be good character sketches, but are sometimes factually unreliable. Frank Harris, his friend and editor, wrote a biography, Oscar Wilde: His Life and Confessions (1916); though prone to exaggeration and sometimes factually inaccurate, it offers a good literary portrait of Wilde. Lord Alfred Douglas wrote two books about his relationship with Wilde. Oscar Wilde and Myself (1914), largely ghost-written by T. W. H. Crosland, vindictively reacted to Douglas's discovery that De Profundis was addressed to him and defensively tried to distance him from Wilde's scandalous reputation. Both authors later regretted their work. Later, in Oscar Wilde: A Summing Up (1939) and his Autobiography he was more sympathetic to Wilde. Of Wilde's other close friends, Robert Sherard; Robert Ross, his literary executor; and Charles Ricketts variously published biographies, reminiscences or correspondence. The first more or less objective biography of Wilde came about when Hesketh Pearson wrote Oscar Wilde: His Life and Wit (1946). In 1954 Wilde's son Vyvyan Holland published his memoir Son of Oscar Wilde, which recounts the difficulties Wilde's wife and children faced after his imprisonment. It was revised and updated by Merlin Holland in 1989.

Oscar Wilde, a critical study by Arthur Ransome was published in 1912. The book only briefly mentioned Wilde's life, but subsequently Ransome (and The Times Book Club) were sued for libel by Lord Alfred Douglas. In April 1913 Douglas lost the libel action after a reading of De Profundis refuted his claims.

Richard Ellmann wrote his 1987 biography Oscar Wilde, for which he posthumously won a National (USA) Book Critics Circle Award in 1988and a Pulitzer Prize in 1989. The book was the basis for the 1997 film Wilde, directed by Brian Gilbert and starring Stephen Fry as the title character.

Neil McKenna's 2003 biography, The Secret Life of Oscar Wilde, offers an exploration of Wilde's sexuality. Often speculative in nature, it was widely criticised for its pure conjecture and lack of scholarly rigour. Thomas Wright's Oscar's Books (2008) explores Wilde's reading from his childhood in Dublin to his death in Paris. After tracking down many books that once belonged to Wilde's Tite Street library (dispersed at the time of his trials), Wright was the first to examine Wilde's marginalia.

Later on, I think everyone will recognise his achievements; his plays and essays will endure. Of course, you may think with others that his personality and conversation were far more wonderful than anything he wrote, so that his written works give only a pale reflection of his power. Perhaps that is so, and of course, it will be impossible to reproduce what is gone forever.

Robert Ross, 23 December 1900

In 2018, Matthew Sturgis' "Oscar: A Life," was published in London. The book incorporates rediscovered letters and other documents and is the most extensively researched biography of Wilde to appear since 1988.

Parisian literati, also produced several biographies and monographs on him. André Gide wrote In Memoriam, Oscar Wilde and Wilde also features in his journals. Thomas Louis, who had earlier translated books on Wilde into French, produced his own L'esprit d'Oscar Wilde in 1920. Modern books include Philippe Jullian's Oscar Wilde, and L'affaire Oscar Wilde, ou, Du danger de laisser la justice mettre le nez dans nos draps (The Oscar Wilde Affair, or, On the Danger of Allowing Justice to put its Nose in our Sheets) by Odon Vallet, a French religious historian. (Source: Wikipedia)

NOTABLE WORKS

ESSAYS

"The Decay of Lying" First published in Nineteenth Century (1889), republished in Intentions (1891).

"Pen, Pencil and Poison" First published in the Fortnightly Review (1889), republished in Intentions (1891).

"The Soul of Man under Socialism" First published in the Fortnightly Review (1891), republished in The Soul of Man (1895), privately printed.

Intentions (1891) Wilde revised his dialogues on aesthetic subjects for publication in this volume, which comprises:

- "The Critic as Artist"
- "The Decay of Lying"
- "Pen, Pencil and Poison"
- "The Truth of Masks"

"Phrases and Philosophies for the Use of the Young" first published in the Oxford student magazine The Chameleon, December 1894)

"A Few Maxims For The Instruction Of The Over-Educated" First published, anonymously, in the 1894 November 17 issue of Saturday Review.

FICTION

Novel

The Picture of Dorian Gray (1890/1891). The first version of "The Picture of Dorian Gray" was published, in a form highly edited by the magazine, as the lead story in the July 1890 edition of Lippincott's Monthly Magazine. Wilde published the longer and revised version in book form in 1891, with an added preface.

Stories

"The Portrait of Mr. W. H." (1889)

The Happy Prince and Other Tales (1888, a collection of fairy tales) consisting of:

- "The Happy Prince"
- "The Nightingale and the Rose"
- "The Selfish Giant"
- "The Devoted Friend"
- "The Remarkable Rocket"

A House of Pomegranates (1891, fairy tales)

Lord Arthur Savile's Crime and Other Stories (1891) Including "The Canterville Ghost" first published in periodical form in 1887.

Complete Short Fiction. Penguin Classics, 2003. Edited with an Introduction and Notes by Ian Small. Contains all works listed above plus Poems in Prose (1894) and one very short 'Elder-tree' (fragment).

POEMS

Ravenna (1878) Winner of the Newdigate Prize.

Poems (1881) Wilde's collection of poetry and first publication.

The Sphinx (1894)

Poems in Prose (1894)

The Ballad of Reading Gaol (1898)

PLAYS

Vera; or, The Nihilists (1880)

The Duchess of Padua (1883)

Lady Windermere's Fan (1892)

A Woman of No Importance (1893)

Salomé (French version) (1893, first performed in Paris 1896)

Salomé: A Tragedy in One Act: Translated from the French of Oscar Wilde by Lord Alfred Douglas, illustrated by Aubrey Beardsley (1894)

An Ideal Husband (1895) (text)

The Importance of Being Earnest (1895) (text)

La Sainte Courtisane and A Florentine Tragedy Fragmentary. First published 1908 in Methuen's Collected Works

(Dates are dates of first performance, which approximate better to the probable date of composition than dates of publication.)

The Importance of Being Earnest and Other Plays. Penguin Classics, 2000. Edited with an Introduction, Commentaries and Notes by Richard Allen Cave. Contains all from above save the first two. Salome is in English.

As an appendix there is one excised scene from The Importance of Being Earnest.

POSTHUMOUS (PREVIOUSLY UNPUBLISHED)

De Profundis (Written 1895-97, in Reading Gaol). Expurgated edition published 1905; suppressed portions 1913, expanded version in The Letters of Oscar Wilde (1962).

The Rise of Historical Criticism (Written while at college) First published in 1905 (Sherwood Press, Hartford, CT) privately printed. Reprinted in Miscellanies, the last volume of the First Collected Edition (1908).

The First Collected Edition (Methuen & Co., 14 volumes) appeared in 1908 and contained many previously unpublished works.

The Second Collected Edition (Methuen & Co., 12 volumes) appeared in installments between 1909–11 and contained several other unpublished works.

The Letters of Oscar Wilde (Written 1868-1900) Published in 1962. Republished as The Complete Letters of Oscar Wilde (2000), with letters discovered since 1962, and new annotations by Merlin Holland.

The Women of Homer (Written 1876, while at college). First published in Oscar Wilde: The Women of Homer (2008) by The Oscar Wilde Society.

The Philosophy of Dress First published in The New-York Tribune (1885), published for the first time in book form in Oscar Wilde On Dress (2013).

MISATTRIBUTED

Teleny, or The Reverse of the Medal (Paris, 1893) has been attributed to Wilde, but its authorship is unclear. One theory is that it was a combined effort by several of Wilde's friends, which he may have edited.

Constance On September 14, 2011, Wilde's grandson Merlin Holland contested Wilde's claimed authorship of this play entitled Constance, scheduled to open that week in the King's Head Theatre. It was not, in fact, "Oscar Wilde's final play," as its producers were claiming. Holland said Wilde did sketch out the play's scenario in 1894, but "never wrote a word" of it, and that "it is dishonest to foist this on the public." The Artistic Director Adam Spreadbury-Maher of the King's Head Theatre and producer of Constance pointed out that Wilde's son, Vyvyan Holland, wrote in 1954, "a significant amount of the dialogue (of Constance) bears the authentic stamp of my father's hand". There is further proof that the developed scenario that Constance was reconstituted from was written by Wilde between 1897 and his death in 1900, rather than the 1894 George Alexander scenario which Merlin Holland quotes.

CPSIA information can be obtained
at www.ICGtesting.com
Printed in the USA
LVHW010009180820
663425LV00003B/405